"The teen drama is center-cou___ ___s
and sub-plots to fill a few epis___
—*Ebony* magazine on *Drama High: Courtin Jayd*

"You'll definitely feel for Jayd Jackson, the bold sixteen-year-old Compton, California, junior at the center of keep-it-real Drama High stories."
—*Essence* magazine on *Drama High: Jayd's Legacy*

"Edged with comedy and a provoking street-savvy plot line, Compton native and Drama High author L. Divine writes a fascinating story capturing the voice of young black America."
—*The Cincinnati Herald* on the *Drama High Series*

"Filled with all the elements that make for a good book—young love, non-stop drama and a taste of the supernatural, it is sure to please."
—THE RAWSISTAZ Reviewers on *Drama High: The Fight*

". . . A captivating look at teen life."
—Harriet Klausner on *Drama High: The Fight*

"If you grew up on a steady diet of saccharine *Sweet Valley* novels and think there aren't enough books specifically for African American teens, you're in luck."
—*Prince George's Sentinel* on *Drama High: The Fight*

"Through a healthy mix of book smarts, life experiences, and down-to-earth flavor, L. Divine has crafted a well-nuanced coming-of-age tale for African-American youth."
—*The Atlanta Voice* on *Drama High: The Fight*

"*Drama High* has it all . . . fun, fast, addictive."
—Cara Lockwood, bestselling author of *Moby Clique*

Also by L. Divine

THE FIGHT

SECOND CHANCE

JAYD'S LEGACY

FRENEMIES

LADY J

COURTIN' JAYD

HUSTLIN'

KEEP IT MOVIN'

HOLIDAZE

Published by Kensington Publishing Corporation

Drama High, Vol. 10

CULTURE CLASH

L. Divine

KENSINGTON PUBLISHING CORP.
www.kensingtonbooks.com

ISBN-13: 978-0-7582-3111-6
ISBN-10: 0-7582-3111-3

First Kensington Trade Paperback Printing: February 2010

10 9 8 7 6 5

Printed in the United States of America

To my stepmother, Enola Thompson-Logan, who always sent me home with something sweet to eat. And to my stepfather, Ricky Haskin, who always brought us groceries when he was courting my mother. The universe has blessed me twice with stepparents who love me like their own child. You both are a blessing, and I am eternally grateful for your love and support.

And a very special thank-you to Lauren Cherrington, a good friend of my mother's who let me sleep on her couch when my daughter and I needed a place to stay. Your generosity helped us through a very difficult period, and for that I will always be grateful. To our midwives: Jane and Sheila. We were from very different cultures and backgrounds, but our present is the same. I can't thank you enough for your compassion, patience, and open hearts. And to Lana Brown, for being the most sincere homegirl I've known in a long, long time. Welcome to mamahood, Ms. Brown!

ACKNOWLEDGMENTS

To my publisher, Dafina/Kensington—thank you for your continued faith in the series. Ten down, thirty-four to go! To my agent, Brendan Deneen—thank you for taking my smack talking and turning it into progressive action. To my readers—thank you always for supporting Jayd and her stories. And to my babies—thank you for giving me the strength to live our culture freely.

The Crew

Jayd

A sassy sixteen-year-old from Compton, California, who comes from a long line of Louisiana conjure women. She is the only one in her lineage born with brown eyes and a caul. Her grandmother appropriately named her "Jayd," which is also the name her grandmother took on in her days as a voodoo queen in New Orleans. She lives with her grandparents, four uncles, and her cousin Jay. Jayd is in all AP classes and visits her mother on the weekend. She has a tense relationship with her father, whom she sees occasionally, and has never-ending drama in her life, whether at school or home.

Mama/Lynn Mae

When Jayd gets in over her head, her grandmother, Mama, is always there to help her. A full-time conjure woman with magical green eyes and a long list of both clients and haters, Mama also serves as Jayd's teacher, confidante, and protector.

Mom/Lynn Marie

At thirty-something years old, Lynn Marie would never be mistaken for a mother of a teenager. Jayd's mom is definitely all that and with her green eyes, she keeps the men guessing. Able to talk to Jayd telepathically, Lynn Marie is always there when Jayd needs her.

Netta

The owner of Netta's Never Nappy Beauty Shop, Netta is Mama's best friend, business partner, and godsister in their religion. She also serves as a godmother to Jayd, who works part-time at Netta's Shop.

Esmeralda

Mama's nemesis and Jayd's nightmare, this next-door neighbor is anything but friendly. She relocated to Compton from Louisiana around the same time Mama did and has been a thorn in Mama's side ever since. She continuously causes trouble for Mama and Jayd. Esmeralda's cold blue eyes have powers of their own, although not nearly as powerful as Mama's.

Rah

Rah is Jayd's first love from junior high school, who has come back into her life when a mutual friend, Nigel, transfers from Rah's high school (Westingle) to South Bay. He knows everything about her and is her spiritual confidant. Rah lives in Los Angeles but grew up with his grandparents in Compton like Jayd. He loves Jayd fiercely but has a girlfriend who refuses to go away (Trish) and a baby-mama (Sandy). Rah is a hustler by necessity and a music producer by talent. He takes care of his younger brother, Kamal, and holds the house down while his dad is locked up and his mother strips at a local club.

Misty

The word "frenemies" was coined for this former best friend of Jayd's. Misty has made it her mission to sabotage Jayd any way she can. Living around the corner from Jayd, she has the unique advantage of being an original hater from the neighborhood and at school.

KJ

He's the most popular basketball player on campus, Jayd's ex-boyfriend, and Misty's current boyfriend. Ever since he and Jayd broke up, he's made it his personal mission to persecute her.

Nellie

One of Jayd's best friends, Nellie is the prissy princess of the crew. She is also dating Chance, even though it's Nigel she's really feeling. Nellie made history at South Bay by becoming the first Black Homecoming princess and has let the crown go to her head.

Mickey

The gangster girl of Jayd's small crew, she and Nellie are best friends but often at odds with each other, mostly because Nellie secretly wishes she could be more like Mickey. A true hood girl, she loves being from Compton, and her man with no name is a true gangster. Mickey and Nigel have quickly become South Bay High's newest couple.

Jeremy

A first for Jayd, Jeremy is her white ex-boyfriend who also happens to be the most popular cat at South Bay. Rich, tall, and extremely handsome, Jeremy's witty personality and good conversation keep Jayd on her toes and give Rah a run for his money—literally.

Mickey's Man

Never using his name, Mickey's original boyfriend is a trouble-maker and always hot on Mickey's trail. Always in and out of jail, Mickey's man is notorious in her hood for being a coldhearted gangster, and loves to be in control. He also has a thing for Jayd, but Jayd can't stand to be anywhere near him.

Nigel

The new quarterback on the block, Nigel is a friend of Jayd's from junior high and also Rah's best friend, making Jayd's world even smaller at South Bay High. Nigel is the star football player and dumped his ex-girlfriend at Westingle (Tasha) to be with his new baby-mama-to-be, Mickey. Jayd is caught up in the mix as a friend to them both, but her loyalty lies with Nigel because she's known him longer and he's always had her back.

Chance

The rich, white hip-hop kid of the crew, Chance is Jayd's drama homie and Nellie's boyfriend, if you let him tell it. He used to have a crush on Jayd and now has turned his attention to Nellie.

Bryan

The youngest of Mama's children and Jayd's favorite uncle, Bryan is a dj by night and works at the local grocery store during the day. He's also an acquaintance of both Rah and KJ from playing ball around the hood. Bryan often gives Jayd helpful advice about her problems with boys and hating girls alike. Out of all of Jayd's uncles, Bryan gives her grandparents the least amount of trouble.

Jay

Jay is more like an older brother to Jayd than her cousin. Like Jayd, he lives with Mama but his mother (Mama's youngest daughter) left him when he was a baby and never returned. He doesn't know his father and attends Compton High. He and Jayd often cook together and help Mama around the house.

CULTURE CLASH

Prologue

This weekend was the first one in a long time I spent hanging with my crew. After our hellish holidays it was nice being back to normal with my friends. Well, all except for my ex Rah. He's completely lost his mind if he thinks allowing his daughter's mother, Sandy, to be under house arrest at his house is the way to go. If it weren't for his daughter, I know he would've had no problem letting her trifling ass be prosecuted to the full extent of the law for stealing his grandfather's car.

I just got my conditioner set in my hair for the next thirty minutes. I feel like cooking a big breakfast this morning, but it'll be nothing like the spread Mama made for me yesterday. My memory's still coming back from our collective vision quest Friday evening. I walk into the kitchen and check the fridge for some food. As usual, there's nothing in here to cook. Damn. I hope there's at least some grits in the cabinet. My mom loves hot cereal and so do I.

I check the cabinet and find what I'm looking for, but not before I'm interrupted by someone at the front door. Who's this knocking so early on a Sunday morning? Maybe it's my neighbor Shawntrese wanting to get her hair done before church. I look through the peephole and see Jeremy, my ex, looking back at me. What's he doing here?

"We're making this pop-up thing a habit, aren't we?" I say through the door, unlocking the multiple bolts and letting him in. Jeremy has seen me look all kinds of ways. Now he gets to see me with my plastic shower cap on and I could not care less. That's what he gets for coming by unannounced.

"Good morning to you, too, Lady J. I had to come check on you since you're not returning calls," he says, walking inside and kissing me on the forehead, but not before he looks at my shower cap and shakes his head in amusement. I haven't even checked my phone this morning. I passed out when I came home from Nigel's last night and put my phone on silent mode to make sure I stayed that way.

"You want some grits?" I ask, sashaying back into the kitchen to finish cooking my breakfast. I open the freezer and find some protein to accompany my meal. Thank God for frozen food. Who knows how long these turkey sausages have been in here. In my opinion, they still look good enough to eat.

"What's a grit?" Jeremy asks, as serious as a heart attack. I turn around and look at him, shocked he's unfamiliar with one of our staple foods. He's a white boy, so I guess he's not familiar with chitlins and pig's feet either, although I haven't had either one of those since I was a child.

"How can you *not* know what grits are? Your mother's from the South." I gesture for Jeremy to sit at the dining room table while I get out the necessary tools needed to cook. I put water in both the pot and the skillet, ready to heat this small kitchen up.

"Yeah, but she doesn't cook everything Southern. My dad's Jewish, remember? Some things we never got accustomed to, a grit being one of them."

"It's not 'a grit.' You don't just eat one," I say, smiling at my silly friend. "And it's like porridge made out of ground corn. Interested?" I begin pouring the white grains into the measuring cup, waiting for his response. From the look on his face, I'd say the answer is no.

"I'll pass." His loss. I pour the cereal slowly into the boiling water and check on my sausages cooking in the skillet. This is going to be a slamming meal. "So, how was the dance?"

"It was okay. I didn't stay for long," I say, mixing the cereal until it's thick and smooth. I reach back into the refrigerator and pull out the butter. I take a knife out of the dish drainer and put about a tablespoon of butter into the grits and then sprinkle in some salt. All I need now is brown sugar to make this meal perfect. I have about five minutes before I need to rinse the conditioner out of my hair. I hope Jeremy wasn't expecting my undivided attention this morning because I'm all about me right now.

"And how was your Valentine's Day?" he asks as I pour the grits onto a plate and place the sausages next to the cereal. I sit across from Jeremy at the table ready to dig in.

"It was cool. I chilled with the crew, nothing special. And on Friday night I was busy with my family, so I was glad for the session last night," I say, offering Jeremy a sausage. He takes it. Something about Jeremy's eyes tells me that I'm missing something here.

"You were so busy you couldn't respond to my text about plans we had for the holiday?" His text? I forgot all about him asking me to be his valentine and about the stupid movie he wanted us to go see. But I can't tell him the truth about why I didn't remember until just now.

"You seem to pick and choose your holidays, Jeremy. I'm sorry I was caught up, and I told you I didn't want to see a horror movie anyway, especially not one as demeaning as the one you chose." I continue eating without apology. If I told him that me, my mother, and my grandmother were busy fighting off Mama's neighbor Esmeralda and my frenemy Misty in the spirit world because they were trying to steal my dreams, I don't think he'd believe me.

"How is a movie about voodoo dolls and shit demeaning to you, unless you're a voodoo witch?" I stop in mid-bite and look into Jeremy's eyes, now full of anger. He's about to piss me and the women in my lineage off if we don't end this conversation right now.

"It's priestess, not witch." Did I just say that out loud? From the look in Jeremy's pretty blues, I guess I did.

"What's the difference?" he asks, taking another sausage from my near-empty plate. I can feel the conditioner in my hair losing its minty tingle, indicating it's about time for my rinse.

"What's the difference? I know you know better than that, Jeremy," I say, finishing the last few bites of my breakfast. "A witch stems from European Wicca beliefs. Voodoo is African, and we are priests and priestesses, not sorcerers, witches, or any other name you might want to call us by." I know Jeremy loves a good debate, but he can save it for our fourth period class tomorrow afternoon. This is not a conversation I want to have with him right now.

"We? Us? Is there something you're not telling me, Jayd?" Some things he'll never understand and I'm not in the mood to teach him.

"Yes, there is, and I'm going to continue not telling you as long as you have an attitude about it." I look at the wall clock and realize I've gone over by one minute on my conditioner. "I have to rinse my hair. I'll be right back," I say, wiping my mouth with a napkin before rising to head back into the bathroom where I've set up hair shop.

"Whatever, Jayd. Call me when you're ready to be straight with me, without the attitude." Jeremy gets up from the table and walks out of the apartment. What the hell just happened here? And why is he accusing me of having an attitude when he's the one acting like a three year-old? Whatever the reason, it can wait until tomorrow, unlike my hair. I should've never answered the door. Maybe I can rinse away some of his negativity with my conditioner and start fresh tomorrow—no drama included.

~ 1 ~
Black Girls

*"Light skin, dark skin, my Asian persuasion/
I got them all, that's why these girls out here hatin'."*

—JANET JACKSON

For once, it's good to be back at school. Stepping out of my car, I notice the air feels new this morning. I guess it's because all of the bad things Misty did were undone when I took back my dreams, including me snatching her weaved head up, which resulted in me going to counseling even though it won't go on my school record because no one remembers. It's nice to have received the benefits of the mandatory week of anger management counseling I had to endure without suffering the consequences. It's also nice that Nellie, Mickey, and I are speaking again. I need my girls to make it through the long days at South Bay High.

"What's up, bitch?" Nellie asks as I approach my girls in the main hall. Now that I'm driving myself instead of taking the bus, I'm managing mornings better, so I don't arrive on campus so early. And Nellie's back to getting a ride with Mickey, as it should be.

"Who you calling a bitch?" I ask, looking around for someone else. I know she's not talking to me or Mickey, because those are definitely fighting words where we come from.

"You, bitch." If it weren't for the smile on Nellie's face I would think she was serious.

"We don't do that," Mickey says, correcting our girl. She

rolls her eyes at me and smiles, knowing how bougie Nellie can be.

"But Laura and her girls say that to each other all the time." I wish we could have stopped Nellie from associating with the ASB clique, but that happened before Misty lost her damn mind. "It's a term of endearment."

"Not for us it's not," I say, walking with my girls from Mickey's locker to mine. The warning bell for first period rings in the buzzing hall, putting the fear of detention in everyone present, especially me. With Mr. Adewale as my new first period teacher, my days of excused tardies from my former Spanish teacher/football coach are over. Mr. A is serious about his shit, and I'm serious about staying on his good side.

"What's so bad about calling your homegirl a bitch if it's said with the utmost love and respect?" Nellie asks. Mickey and I look at our girl and shake our heads in disbelief. Nellie's clueless on certain subjects, and the black girl code of etiquette is one of them.

"Look at Laura and her girls and then look at us," I say, gesturing to the bitch crew entering the hall from the main office. "Now you tell me what's the difference." I open my backpack and switch out my books. I need to clean my locker, but I'm afraid of throwing anything away, especially after what happened last time. Misty went through my trash and found a note, trying to help incriminate me for forging an excuse for Mickey and Nigel when they ditched school, which is what got us into trouble in the first place. I'm glad that's all behind us, but I'm not putting anything past Misty after what we just went through.

"They're rich and we're not. Well, y'all aren't, but you feel me," Nellie says, flipping her straight hair over her right shoulder.

"You ain't balling either, Miss Thang," Mickey says, checking Nellie. I'm so glad we're back to "us" I don't know what

to do. Dealing with them one-on-one was too much for a sistah to handle.

"We're black, Nellie, and they are not. We don't go around
calling each other bitches, hoes, or any other derogatory
term, because of the history attached to the words for us and
our ancestors." I slam my locker door shut and begin speed-
walking toward my first period, with my girls in tow. They
can afford to stroll into their class late, unlike me.

"Jayd, you really should let go of all of that negativity. History's in the past. Leave it there." I stop in my tracks and stare
at my girl. Mickey laughs at my reaction, but I know she feels
part of what I'm saying. My ancestors are probably crying
right now, they're so mad.

"Nellie, have you ever heard us refer to each other as
bitches and then hug afterwards?" I'm liable to smack a female instead of embrace her if she calls me out of my name.

"Hell to the no," Mickey says, taking a pack of Skittles out
of her purse and eating them. Mickey looks at Nellie with a
dare in her eyes and Nellie returns the stare. My girls are
crazy. I'm just glad we're all on the same side again. As small
as the black population is on this campus, we can't afford to
be at odds with each other. It's bad enough the three of us
don't get along with the South Central clique, where the
other twenty-plus black students chill. Without each other,
Nellie, Mickey, and I would truly be lost. I remember that feeling, even if my girls don't, and it was a lonely existence.

"Y'all are too sensitive. It's not that big a deal," Nellie says
as we exit the main hall. The morning air feels different with
spring approaching. I love this time of year and not just because my birthday's next month. Something about warm sea-
sons makes school—and life in general—more pleasant.

"Good morning, ladies," Nigel says, greeting us all as we
walk across the courtyard. He puts his arm across Mickey's
shoulders and falls in step with us.

"Good morning," we say in unison. Even with the semester change, the three of them still share most of the same classes. At first I wasn't sure about having a general ed class, but it hasn't been that bad, with the exception of having to deal with Misty and KJ. Now that our crew is solid, I know it'll be live in fourth period for the remainder of the semester.

"What up, dog?" Chance says, greeting Nigel before saying hi to us. He kisses Nellie on the lips and then big ups Mickey and me. "Good session this weekend, man."

"Yes, it was," Nigel says, reminding me of the last conversation I had with Rah on Saturday. I haven't talked to him since I found out his baby-mama is his new roommate. He's called and texted me a million times since then, and he can keep on blowing my cell up. Mama says if I don't have anything nice to say I shouldn't say anything at all. And whatever comes out of my mouth won't be good for Rah, so I'm going to avoid cussing him out for as long as I possibly can.

"Bye, bitches," Nellie says, running toward their first period class ahead of Mickey and Nigel, with Chance right behind her. She thinks she's funny but she's not. Calling one another bitches is something Nellie needs to reserve for her white friends. We black girls are not feeling that shit in the least.

"That's your friend," Mickey says. Nigel laughs at his girl, and I can't help but do the same.

"But you've known her longer," I add. We make it to my Spanish class, where the door is wide open. Mr. Adewale doesn't count you as present unless you're sitting at your desk when the bell stops ringing. We have about a minute to go before the final bell rings, officially starting the school day.

Mr. A looks up at me from the stack of papers on his desk. His smile is reserved, but I feel more caution in his eyes than usual. Maybe Ms. Toni had the same conversation she had with me about him and me associating with each other on a friendly basis. I think she's overreacting, but what can I say? I know how these folks up here are, and with them being the only two teachers of color on the lily-white faculty, I can't say that I blame her. I just wish she had a little more faith in me.

"Don't remind me," Mickey says. As she takes her backpack off of her shoulders and passes it to Nigel to carry, I notice a new picture keychain hanging with our old photo from homecoming.

"What's this?" I ask, taking a look at the photo. It's a picture of Mickey, Nigel, Chance, Nellie, Rah, and me from the Valentine's Day dance last Friday.

"What do you mean? You have the same one, remember?" she says, fingering the same set of photos hanging from my backpack. I'm glad there's a picture to prove we were all in attendance at the dance because I don't remember any of it—another side effect from the dream sharing thanks to Misty. And from the smiles on our faces it looks like we had a good time.

"My bad, girl. You know I'm sleep deprived." Luckily I'm not anymore, but I have to blame my memory loss on something, and that's part of the truth.

"We'll see you in third period, Jayd. We have a meeting with the principal at break," Nigel says as the final bell rings. I glance at Mr. A, who has his pencil and attendance sheet ready to mark the latecomers.

"Holla," Mickey says as she and her man casually stroll toward their first-period class. I missed Mickey being on the main campus briefly before I went back and changed the past, including Mickey deciding to take the principal's suggestion for her to attend the continuation school across the football field. She talked with Nigel about the administration bullying her, and they've decided to stand up to the powers that be, together. I'm glad she decided to stay and fight. We have to stick together in this wilderness. Otherwise, they will pluck us out one by one, with us girls being the first on their exit list. I'm not leaving this campus until I have a diploma in my hand, and I hope Mickey feels the same way.

First period's not as chill as it used to be with Mr. Donald, but with Mr. Adewale we're actually learning Spanish. Even the new kid on the block, Emilio, is impressed by Mr. Adewale's command of the foreign language. I don't know why Emilio's in Spanish class since he can speak his first tongue fluently. But I enjoy the attention he gives me.

Emilio and I didn't get to talk much in first period because Mr. A decided it would be fun to have a pop quiz on Chapter One, which he told us to study thoroughly last week. It was a challenge, but I think I did okay. I can't speak for the rest of the class. But when we walked out a few moments ago, I heard other students calling Mr. A everything but a child of God.

"Miss Jackson, please pass these out for me when you get settled," Mrs. Malone says as I walk into my second-period class, pointing to a stack of papers at the corner of her desk. I hang my backpack on the corner of my chair and claim the papers while the rest of the class files in before the bell rings.

"What's this?" Alia, my favorite English classmate, asks. "Damn, another paper already? The semester just started a couple of weeks ago." I agree. But there's no rest for the weary and we are definitely worn out on our AP track. After the AP exams in a few weeks, everything will hopefully calm down.

"Oh, Miss Cole," Mrs. Malone says to Alia. "You're a very talented writer. You shouldn't have any complaints." She rises from her seat as the bell rings and props herself up on the corner of her desk, ready to begin class. I place the last handout on my desk and sit down next to Alia, who's already started copying the daily notes from the board.

"Good morning, class. Today's quote is from one of my fa-

vorite writers, John Updike. Charlotte, would you mind recit-
ing it, please?" The bland-looking white girl puts on her glasses
and reads from the whiteboard. Out of all the students in this
class, she's my least favorite.

" 'Dreams come true; without that possibility, nature would
not incite us to have them.' " The class continues copying the
words from the board while reflecting on what was just said.
Mrs. Malone has a peaceful order to her class that I look forward to on a daily basis. After a few moments of silence, everyone puts their pens down and waits for our teacher to speak.

"Do you think this quote is true, that dreams really do
come true?" After the question lingers in the air for a moment,
I take the initiative and answer, since everyone else is apparently still asleep this morning.

"Yes, I do. But not because he said it." I already know from
our reading of some of his short stories that Updike is some
old white man. And most of the ideas he has aren't really that
original. Mrs. Malone looks at me knowingly, ready to challenge my opinions. That's why I like her. For a middle-aged
white woman, she's pretty cool when it comes to literary stuff.

"Dig deeper, Jayd," she says, repeating her mantra. If I had
a dime for every time she said that I'd be a rich woman by
now.

"Well, take for example the dream of becoming the first
black president. If Obama hadn't had the thought, he wouldn't
have been able to picture it as his reality," I say, causing most
eyes to roll. It's Black History Month, but you wouldn't know
it at this school until the end of the month. Every year they
hold a voluntary assembly during lunch, merging the an-
nouncement of the Cultural Awareness Festival with the end
of Black History Month. Works my nerves every year. Out of
protest, I usually don't attend.

"Good, Jayd, but go even further than that. And take race
out of it, because I know that's what you're thinking." Easy

for her to say. I hate when Mrs. Malone pretends she can read our minds, even if she's right. Who does she think she is, Mama?

"I don't agree with Updike," Charlotte says. "First off, I think he's wrong to say that nature incites us to have dreams. I think it's our daily experiences that make us dream. Nature has nothing to do with that." I marvel at Charlotte's ignorance. Some people are so clueless.

"How can nature have nothing to with that, if it's a daily experience? Nature is in everything, including our daily lives." The rest of the class watch Charlotte and me go back and forth in a tennis match of words. For them, it's nothing new. Charlotte and I are the most vocal participants on our AP track.

"Jayd, please. You think nature really gives a damn whether or not you dream?" She can cuss in class all day. And as long as she doesn't go too far with it, Mrs. Malone won't check her. Now let me say some shit like that and I'll automatically be reprimanded for being the angry black girl in the room, fo sho.

"Here we go," Alia whispers to me, making me smile. If it weren't for her comic relief, I'd probably tolerate Charlotte's ass much less than I already do.

"Nature controls grass and trees and whatnot, not our psyches. My daddy says that dreams are merely an indication that we have achieved deep sleep—rapid eye movement—nothing more." Charlotte's father is some pseudo shrink who's famous for his books on the power of the mind to help you get rich. She thinks she's hot shit. I can't stand her ass on a good day.

"Well, your daddy's wrong," I say, making the class laugh—all except for Charlotte, of course. "Nature's in all things. We can't be separate from creation because we are a part of it, including our minds."

"That's a very interesting perspective, Jayd. Why do you think we are a part of nature?" Mrs. Malone asks, looking at me curiously like I'm about to say something profound.

"Because we didn't create ourselves. And not only that, every element in the Earth can be found inside of our bodies. We are mostly water, so is the Earth." Before I can continue, Charlotte interrupts my flow.

"Because we are part of the evolutionary process doesn't mean that nature controls our thoughts. That's such a primitive idea." Both the rude interruption and the insult warrant a beat-down.

"Excuse me?" I say, my attitude moving into my neck. "Did you just call me primitive?" Mama still doesn't shop at Ikea to this day because they described one of their kente prints as primitive. Not African, but primitive, like they couldn't find any other word in the entire English language to accurately describe the West African pattern.

"I called your thought process primitive; simplistic, passé, ancient," Charlotte says, angering me more with every synonym for the offensive word that slips from her tongue. I envision slapping the taste out of her mouth, spit flying everywhere, and wiping that smug smile clear off her face.

"Sometimes simple is more complex than we give it credit for." I know Mrs. Malone thinks she's helping me, but now I feel even more offended.

"Nothing about nature is simple, dreaming included." The steadiness in my voice stills the excited room and scares me a little, too. I'm so sick of defending myself against these white folks up here. It's both mentally and spiritually exhausting. And what's even more annoying is that they don't get how ingrained their racism is.

"Whatever, Jayd. Some of us read and educate ourselves without just shooting off our opinions. I can recommend a few valid references if you'd like to study the topic in depth."

I look at Charlotte and imagine her head blowing up, her red hair flying all over the spacious classroom. Noting the heat rising to my cheeks, Mrs. Malone takes the topic over and shifts gears.

"Okay, girls, back to your corners," Mrs. Malone says, focusing her attention on the handout. She may be joking, but that's exactly how I feel every day on this campus: I'm in a boxing ring fighting an opponent I'll never be allowed to defeat.

"As you can see, your next paper's topic will be chosen from the short story 'A & P' by John Updike, thus this morning's quote. Please turn to page two hundred in your textbooks." We dutifully open our books and read in silence.

I can barely concentrate on the text, I'm so heated from our previous discussion. I manage to get through the few pages with the rest of the class. Once everyone's finished, Mrs. Malone opens the floor for discussion.

"So, what do you think of Queenie? Was she judged accurately or was he too hard on her?"

"I think attitude says a lot about a person's character." Charlotte thinks she's slick, but I know she's talking about me. "But I think he's more envious than anything, like most jealous people." Now I know this bitch is tripping. With her around it's impossible to get through a discussion without bringing race into it.

"And then some people think that they're all that, when they're not," I respond. "I think that's Queenie and her wannabe crew. Society has allowed Queenie to think she's better than some people simply because of her station in life, which she hasn't even earned. The wealth belongs to Queenie's parents. In essence she has nothing," I say, impressing Mrs. Malone with my reasoning. "Some of us have to actually work for a living and earn our cocky attitudes," I say, thoroughly pissing Charlotte off.

"And some of us have been blessed with good fortune from our parents' hard work." Charlotte and I stare each other down, each ready to pounce if given the chance.

The bell sounds, interrupting our heated discussion just in time. One more minute and Miss Charlotte would've been picking her smart-ass self up from the floor.

"Please reread the text thoroughly. I look forward to receiving your abstracts and outlines on Friday." Before I can gather all of my things, Mrs. Malone takes a seat in the chair next to mine.

"What's up, Mrs. Malone?" I ask, ready to jet. We only have twenty minutes for break and I'm starving. The last thing I want to deal with is another lecture from a teacher about my bad attitude.

"You can't let her get to you, Jayd. In life, you will always meet opposition. And if you walk around with a chip on your shoulder, there will always be someone willing to knock it off."

"I hear you, Mrs. Malone." I don't want to spend any more time in here than I have to. And if agreeing with everything she says will get me out of here faster, I'll do just that.

"Now, I want you to think hard about how you want to approach this paper. Updike has a lot to offer through his writings, even if he is an old white man," Mrs. Malone says, taking the unspoken words right out of my mouth. "I'm looking forward to hearing your thoughts in class tomorrow." Yeah, I'm sure. Mrs. Malone loves probing the mind of the colored girl in the room. I wonder if she treats her Native American husband the same way when they're having a conversation at home.

"Okay. See you in the morning," I say, quickly leaving the classroom. That was five minutes of my personal time wasted. I need to eat now, and get something to snack on for later. We have a drama club meeting at lunch and I want to be in attendance for the entire thing. This semester I intend to take the lead in initiating our performance choices, starting with the Cultural Festival scene we're performing. It's about time we did something with a little more flavor, and I've got just the thing. I've just got to make it through the next two classes without cussing somebody out so I can get to the meeting, for real.

With the spring play auditions around the corner, all of the thespians, including myself, are in rare form preparing monologues for auditions. I've chosen a monologue from *Fences* to showcase my acting talents. I'm also offering it as a play suggestion, even if I know it's asking a lot from the majority white club to even consider performing a black play. But I'm still going to put it out there, just to shake things up a bit. This is our first meeting for the new semester and the main topic on the agenda is the performance for the festival next month, something else I'm auditioning for.

"I move to perform a short scene from *The Crucible*. It was a winner for the Orange County drama festival last year," Seth says, overly hyped about his suggestion. The hell I'm performing another scene as a slave girl.

"I move that we perform a play written by a nonwhite playwright," I say, ready to throw my hat in the ring. "How about *Fences* by August Wilson?" They all look at me, shell-shocked.

"I love that play," Chance says, having my back as usual. It's nice to have an ally in the club who also happens to be our best male lead actor. "I think that's a great idea."

"Jayd, there are no parts for *us* in that script," Seth says. At least he knows the play. Maybe there's hope for him yet.

"There are never any parts for me in any of the scripts that we perform around here on the regular, but that doesn't stop me from performing," I say. And it's true. The vast majority of the plays we perform have a traditionally white cast, but that never stops me from auditioning.

"That's not true. We chose *The Crucible* specifically with you in mind." I thumb through the script Seth hands me, already knowing the plot. I've read the damned play so many times on my own that I could recite Tituba's lines verbatim.

"Yeah, I noticed," I say, throwing the script down on the floor in front of me. If it were Maryse Condé's version of what happened to one of my early ancestors, I might consider the role. But there's no way in hell that I'm accepting this part. "I'm not playing a slave." Matthew, Seth, and Chance look at me, their pale faces turning crimson as they choose how to react to my claim. I know Chance doesn't agree with them about their scene choice, but he still wants me in the play. We work well together and everyone knows it.

"And I'm not playing a black man," Seth says. "What do you want me to do, wear blackface and speak Ebonics?" Seth has gone too far now; that was definitely the wrong thing for him to say.

"Seth, that statement is so ignorant I don't know where to begin. If I wasn't afraid of going to jail I'd beat the hell out of you right where you stand," I say, trying to calm myself down—but it's not going to be easy. I already had to defend myself in English class this morning and now I'm back on the stand, still the only black girl in the crew. Where are my peers when I need them?

"Okay, let's all calm down. No need for beating anyone's ass," Chance says, trying to lighten the mood. But it's too late for that. The bigot is out of the bag and running free all around the drama room. Alia and two other members of the thespian club, Ella and Cameron, walk into the miniature theater and feel the heat.

"Yeah, Jayd, relax. It's just a play," Seth says. I know he's not still talking after that racist remark. It's just a play, my ass.

"How would you feel if every play we chose always had a degrading gay character in it who you were automatically chosen to play because we all know that you're a homosexual?" Seth thinks about what I've said, but still sides with his folks. After all, no one would know he was gay if he didn't open his mouth. He's white first, and we all know the drill.

That's why I'm not really down for the gay rights activists using the Civil Rights Movement as an example for their struggles. I agree we should all be able to live as we see fit, but some of us are freer in society than others because of race first, sexual orientation second.

"What's going on here?" Alia asks, making herself comfortable in one of the seats across the room with the other two girls sitting near by.

"Jayd's pissed because we want to do *The Crucible* for our spring play and perform a scene from it for the Cultural Festival, too," Matt says, throwing his pen down on the floor in front of him, he's so frustrated with the topic at hand. Like Jeremy, he's not the confrontational type. Maybe it's all the water in their ears from surfing that usually keeps them so mellow.

"Oh, that's a great idea. I love Arthur Miller's writing." Cameron would love it. She's as much a puritan as any of the characters in the play.

"So what's the problem?" Ella asks, already bored with the conversation. She takes a mirror out of her Dooney & Bourke purse and perfects her flawless makeup. The diva of the club, Ella rarely comes to meetings, or class for that matter. Apparently her agent keeps her busy with auditions during the day. She's a proud card–carrying SAG member, and most of the drama hams around here want to be just like her.

"The problem is that Jayd doesn't want to play Tituba, so who will?" Seth asks, as if the play is now ruined because the token black girl refuses to play the only black role. Oh well.

"Why can't I audition like everyone else and play one of

the other parts? There are more female roles than just the slave," I offer, just to further goad them into another racist confession. I have no intention of playing a Puritan, anymore than they have of playing a slave.

"Oh, Jayd, please. You're always complaining about something or other. Can't you just be happy that you always have a part, especially when there's a black female role? It's yours, hands down," Ella says, never looking up from the compact mirror she's primping in.

"Did you really just say that shit to me?" I ask, rising from my seat, ready to march over and confront her head-on. Before I can, the door to our small room opens, cutting the tension in the air like a knife.

"Hey, what's going on in here? We can hear all of you on the stage," Mrs. Sinclair says, coming in from the main theater to break up our growing disagreement. I thought the drama club was the one clique I could be a part of, and lose myself in a character on a regular basis. But it's times like these I see I'll always be the odd girl out.

"What's going on is that there are some serious racists up in this place and I can't take it anymore," I say, opening my bag of Hot Cheetos in my lap and stuffing my mouth with a handful of the spicy snack. They probably won't help me calm down, but they will momentarily slow me down from talking smack in front of Mrs. Sinclair.

"Oh, Jayd, calm down. You're always so overdramatic about things. I'm sure it's not all that bad," she says, automatically taking their side. I keep eating and they keep talking.

"Well, actually, Mrs. Sinclair, Jayd's got a point," Chance says, coming to my defense. He's my boy even if he's unaware that he should be offended, too because his birth mother is half-black according to one of my dreams. "We do tend to choose plays that favor the majority. How about we try something different?"

"Chance, I can't talk about this now," Mrs. Sinclair says, her hands waving above her frizzy head. Talk about over-dramatic. She's the one teaching me a thing or two. "Whatever you vote for is what we're going to perform, end of discussion," she says, taking the final word back to the stage with her. Seth and Matt look relieved and victorious, knowing the vote is unnecessary. Why do I even try?

"Excuse me. I need some air," I say, rising from my seat and taking my chips with me. Chance follows me out the door as the bell for fifth period rings, ending our meeting anyway.

"Jayd, I'm sorry about those jerks," he says, putting his hands on my shoulders and rubbing them softly. He gives great massages, or used to. Ever since I started dating Jeremy and he and Nellie hooked up, we don't spend much time alone together anymore. I miss my friend. "I wouldn't want to play a witch either."

"She's not a witch. She's a priestess," I say, repeating the same rationale to Chance as I argued with Jeremy this past weekend.

"Okay, priestess," he says, throwing his hands up in mock surrender. "But still, I would take more offense at playing that part of the role than being a slave. History is history."

"But it's a biased view of history, Chance. And by the way, it's captive, not slave," I say. The late bell rings, signaling it's time to get back inside.

"Okay, Jayd, now you're just getting too sensitive about this. I don't know what you want me to say, but I've got your back either way it goes," Chance says, going back into the crowded room ahead of me. Maybe he has a point. How can I get upset at the students when the adults are the ones enforcing the bull that they learn? Mrs. Sinclair didn't even entertain my idea, and she dismissed my disapproval of Seth's suggestion as another case of "black girl rage."

The teachers are the ones I should be mad at, not the

dumb-ass students I have to put up with. Unfortunately, no matter how hot I get, there's really no use in fighting the administration up here. Mrs. Bennett's the only teacher-bitch I can deal with, and she has made the biased rules apparent enough for me. But no matter what, I refuse to allow this school to make me forget who I am and where I come from. And willingly playing the role of a slave is unacceptable to me when I know my ancestors and elders taught me better than that.

~ 2 ~
The Administration

*"They schools ain't teachin' us what we need to know to survive/
They schools don't educate, all they teach the people is lies."*

—DEAD PREZ

I didn't get to chill with my girls yesterday at all because I had to meet with Mrs. Malone about my English paper topic. And being that it was a regular short Tuesday yesterday for teacher's meetings, I had no time to do anything but get to class and sit in my mandatory AP meetings during lunch and break, which are now on Tuesdays and Thursdays until the AP exams are over.

With the AP exams less than two months away, teachers and students alike are feeling the pressure. This is my first year on the AP track, and so far it hasn't been too different from the honors classes I took last year, except for the meetings. Being a sophomore was bliss compared to my junior year. If it weren't for my friends, school would be unbearable, especially now that I have to deal with Mrs. Bennett twice a week. I'm just glad that Mr. Adewale is here full-time now, to balance out the evil Mrs. B's presence in my life.

Speaking of bitches, I talked to Rah briefly about his and his ex Sandy's living situation, and it was less than favorable for me. I'm not sure what to do about loving Rah, and I know he's just trying to do the right thing, but I'm convinced that living with Sandy is not it. How can I get him to understand where I'm coming from without sounding like a jealous hater? Until she's out of his house I can't be in his life the way he wants me to be. In his mind, he and I, along with his daughter, Rahima, could be the perfect teenage family. I don't know what dream world he's living in, but I could never be down with that arrangement as long as Sandy's receiving mail at his address.

I didn't share with Mama this latest development in my soap opera with Rah, but I did tell her about my school drama during her regularly scheduled hair appointment at Netta's shop yesterday afternoon. She and Netta, Mama's best home girl, gave me advice on how to deal with racial injustice on a spiritual level, and also assigned me spirit homework to accompany the verbal lesson. As if I didn't already have enough work to do. Mr. Adewale taking over my Spanish class has been a mixed blessing indeed. I have more studying in that class now than ever before. But luckily most of our homework for debate class is writing responses to the topics discussed in class. There's also some reading, but it's nothing I can't handle.

Now that me and my crew have fourth period together and we're friends again, it's fun being in class with them. And with the topics that Mr. Adewale chooses, there's always plenty for us to argue about. And from the look of the topic on the board, today's no exception.

As soon as we're all settled in our seats, class begins with a bang.

"So, our debate topic for the day deals with race in society. Is America truly a melting pot and, if it is, does race still matter?" Mr. Adewale's good at choosing insightful topics to discuss. It's also interesting being in a general education class, where most of the black students are. I've never been in a class at South Bay where the white students are the minority.

It feels empowering to free up a bit and not be the only black student.

"Hell no, it ain't no melting pot. This ain't nacho cheese," Del says, starting the debate off with a bang.

"It won't become one because you all won't let it," Candace, one of the few white girls in the class, states. She sounds like she could be friends with Jeremy, who looks at her and smiles. Jeremy sits all the way back in his chair and crosses his arms over his chest, ready to watch the sparks fly.

"I don't understand," Emilio says. He sounds so sexy with his Spanish accent. I know most of the females in here would love an opportunity to hear him say their names over and over again.

"We know you don't," KJ says, making him and his boys laugh.

"That's enough, KJ. I told you no disrespect would be allowed in this class at all," Mr. Adewale says, checking KJ once and for all.

"What I mean to say is that I'm curious as to why America would want to melt away the uniqueness of each culture. There's very little individuality in this country, if you ask me."

"Good point, Emilio," Mr. A says proudly. He loves it when his students think before they speak, as he states all the time. "Any counters?"

"Yeah, I've got a counter," Jeremy says, sitting his tall frame erect in his seat, ready to give my new crush a run for his money. "This is one country with one constitution and one people, thus one culture. We can honor the various customs of the people within our society. But America is one melting pot."

"And the people living here should either accept that or roll out." Matt has been pissed with me since our discussion at the drama club meeting the other day. And I see he's chosen our debate class as the perfect forum to vent his frustration.

"But some of the people who are here didn't exactly have a choice in coming to this land, so we should be able to live our culture freely. Isn't that also a part of our constitution?" Emilio looks across the room at me and smiles. Mr. A also smiles at my statement; obviously proud that at least one of us is speaking the truth. Other than Ms. Toni, everyone else in the administration would shudder at my words.

"Oh, here we go with slavery again. It's the end of Black History Month, we know. Can we please move on from the past?" Candace says, sounding like the privileged white girl she is.

"Candace, it's not in the past. That's the point. The racism from times of captivity may have been more blatant, but the institutionalized racism is worse, because everyone can't see it and some people actually choose to be blind," I say, turning my focus to Jeremy. This is an argument we've had many times before and will continue to have as long as he thinks with a stick up his ass about the subject.

"Why are y'all always so angry?" Candace asks, silencing every black student in the previously bustling room. If we weren't afraid of suffering the consequences, I think we would all be down for locking the door and giving her a proper ass-whipping right here and now. But we'll have to settle this battle with our words instead.

"Because we're always referred to as 'y'all,'" I say. For the moment it doesn't matter that Misty, KJ, and I don't get along. Mickey and Shae even look at each other, ready to jump the white girl together if need be. Instantly, all the black students are unified against the others in the room. And they know it. Like my very first week at South Bay High as a sophomore, when a notorious skinhead wore a racist shirt on campus and promptly got his ass beat, we join forces when need be.

"That's why we need a black history class, because y'all fools up here don't know shit about being black," KJ says heatedly. I don't usually have anything nice to say about my pompous ex-boyfriend. But today I'm proud of him.

"We need our own club," I say, speaking the first idea in my head. Mr. Adewale looks at me, his hazel eyes sparkling as if I said exactly what was on his mind, too. The bell rings, momentarily saving the white people in the room from having to discuss the subject any further.

"Good class today, and don't forget to read the next chapter in your textbooks and have a valid response ready for tomorrow's class," Mr. Adewale says, rising from his desk and walking over to where I'm seated, still hot from the conversation. I don't know why I always let these people up here get on my nerves. It's not like the administration would ever teach true tolerance and respect, because they don't have to. According to them, anyone who's not white is the minority in every way, damned with how unjust their melting pot is.

"Jayd, if you're serious about forming your own group, I'll be happy to consider being your adviser."

"I'm very serious," I say, finally putting my textbook in my backpack and rising from my seat, ready to enjoy a relaxing lunch period. I need to cool off, and Jeremy inviting me out for Mexican food is all the chill I need. "It's long overdue." I'm so glad we have another black teacher to join Ms. Toni that I could shout it from the rooftop of the main office. If this were a plantation, the office would definitely be the big house, the classrooms the slave quarters, and the vast majority of the teachers would be the overseers. The problem is that most of these teachers don't see themselves as being racist, and those are the worst kinds of bigots.

"Good," Mr. A says, his eyes still aglow. If I knew suggesting a black club was all it would take to make him look at me like this I would've done it months ago. "Let's all meet during lunch to discuss the idea further," he says, addressing the students still in the room—including Jeremy, who's now making his escape. I guess we won't be having lunch together after all. "We're going to have to be at our best to get approval from the administration to make our club valid. I can even pull in Ms. Toni as a co-adviser if she has time. I'm sure she'd be interested."

"Now?" KJ asks, his fire already dwindling at the mention of sacrificing any of his free time, no matter the cause. And from the heavy sighing from the rest of his crew, I'd say they're feeling just like their leader.

"Yes, now." Mr. A's serious about his shit and so am I. If I can unwillingly give my time to AP, I can certainly give it to my people. "It's my lunch period, too, and I'm willing to give it up if you are." At the risk of sounding like a punk, KJ agrees and we all split to get our food. I know half of the South Central clique won't be in attendance for our first meeting, no matter what KJ decides to do. I can feel him not wanting to join another club, especially with basketball and track practice. But this is necessary, and will do him more good than harm.

"Wish we could, but Mickey and I have a meeting with the administration about her staying on the main campus, baby and all," Nigel says. He sounds like he's dreading it, as well he should. Athlete or not, dealing with the office is never a fun experience.

"Okay. I'm sure your friends will fill you in. Everyone else, let's meet back here in ten minutes," Mr. A says, gathering the homework papers from the empty desks and stacking them neatly on his desk. I follow my friends out to retrieve our lunches and get back here. I don't know about everyone else, but I'm looking forward to this meeting.

Once we're all settled with our lunches in tow, we immediately get down to business. With only thirty minutes left in the lunch period, there's no time to waste. Nigel enters the classroom with a sullen look on his face, and Mickey is nowhere in sight. That can't be good.

"Nigel, what happened to the meeting?" I ask, settling back into my seat, ready to get this meeting underway. I open my bag of Hot Cheetos and begin the smacking fest. I don't know what it is about me and these chips lately, but whatever it is has got me sprung.

"Man, they only let me state my case and then told me to bounce. They'll talk to me about my role in Mickey's pregnancy later." Sounds like some typical divide and conquer bull to me. The last time Mickey and Nigel were in the office together during the ditching investigation, they were tighter than Beyoncé and Jay-Z. But now Nigel's here and my girl's not. Something's definitely wrong with this picture.

"How did Mickey feel about you deserting her?" I ask as Mr. A reclaims his post on the corner of his desk. The rest of the group files in, readjusting themselves in the warm room, ready to reengage in the creation of our new club. I wipe my red fingers on my napkin, take a drink from my water bottle, and continue my smacking. There's a lot of ground to cover, but I'm still going to get my grub on like everyone else. Just as I anticipated, the majority of the class isn't present, but much to my surprise KJ and his crew are here.

"I didn't desert her," Nigel whispers. "And Mickey said she could handle it and that she'll meet us back here when she gets out of the meeting." Nigel won't admit it, but he's scared for our girl. I am, too, especially considering that I've already witnessed what will happen if Mickey leaves the main campus to attend the continuation school on the other side of the football field. She was jealous, paranoid, and made my and Nigel's lives a living hell. I'll be damned if I go there again with her.

"There's power in identification," Mr. Adewale says, his baritone voice silencing our chatter and officially beginning the meeting. "So, what's our group's name?" he asks, taking a drink of his bottled water. He already inhaled his sandwich and apple like it was going out of style. Now he's downing the water so fast it doesn't even look like he's swallowing. I wonder if eating fast comes with being from a long lineage of Ogun priests? Having a warrior as his head orisha or personal path of the creator who is also a great ancestor, must be very different from having a sweet orisha like Oshune crowning your head. Like Mr. A said, it's all in the name.

"Black People United," Money says. I'm actually impressed with his forethought in coming up with the name, especially considering he's always renaming himself something silly. Just last month his name was CMoney. Now he only goes by Money. Next thing I know he'll be calling himself Dime or something else like that. I wonder if he feels more powerful with each incarnation?

"That's a good suggestion," Mr. A. says, writing on the legal pad in front of him. His honey brown skin flexes with each stroke of the pen, making me wish I was the yellow-lined paper in his hands. "Any other suggestions?" he asks, snapping me out of my wishful thoughts.

"How about 'AHP'?" Shae suggests. "It stands for 'Authentic Hood People.'" She gets a good laugh from her South Central crew. Even her quiet man, Tony, lets out a giggle at that name. They're not taking the club seriously. But, unlike me, Mr. Adewale still has hope for them.

"Okay, I'll write that down," Mr. A says, smiling as he scribes. I guess you've got to love our people no matter how ghetto they can be sometimes. "Let's have one more suggestion," he says, looking around the packed room. Half of the black students in the debate class are here. Chance, Emilio, and Alia are also present, solidifying their being down for equality, I assume. Fifteen members is a good start. It's also fewer people to argue with, and that's always a good thing.

"How about 'The African Student Union,'" I add. "Just like the groups on college campuses." KJ automatically rolls his eyes at my suggestion, but Mr. A seems to like it. KJ's probably mad he didn't come up with it himself.

"I think that's a good idea, linking our group to the ones at most universities. There's power in unity," Mr. Adewale says. KJ and his crew eye me like I'm the teacher's pet and that's just fine with me. I'll happily wear that crown.

"I agree," Emilio says, winking at me from across the room. "It's also more inclusive of other African cultures that may not identify themselves as black, and that's important."

"Man, what would you know about being African? Mexico is south of the border, nowhere near Africa last time I looked at a map." Del thinks he's so slick, no matter how dumb he may sound. KJ and Money give their boy dap while Mr. A shakes his head, embarrassed at their behavior.

"I am from Venezuela and I've never been to Mexico," Emilio says, leaning back in his chair and smiling coyly. He's so sexy in a self-assured sort of way. "But I do know there's African blood present in Mexican culture as well." Emilio wears his intelligence for everyone to see, which makes it hard to believe he's only a sophomore. "We are a part of the African diaspora. Maybe you should look more closely at the map next time." The veins in Del's neck are really popping now. If his brown skin weren't a shade darker than my mother's, we'd all be able to see how red-hot he really is. I finish off the last of my lunch, waiting for the next move.

"And maybe you should learn to speak English so that other people understand what you're saying before trying to act black, man," KJ says, coming to his boy's defense—but it's no use. They've been punked by Emilio and we all know it.

"We'll talk about acting black at the next meeting. By the way, everyone needs to think of one good day a week to meet. We'll vote on that next time," Mr. Adewale says, glancing at the wall clock. We only have a few minutes left in our lunch period and we should be able to agree on at least one thing before our first meeting is adjourned. "Let's vote on the name before we go any further. Write down your choice on a piece of paper and put it in here." Mr. Adewale takes an empty coffee mug off his desk and passes it around the room. When everyone's submitted their ballots he counts them and announces the winner.

"The African Student Union," he announces, obviously pleased with the result. I'm surprised they voted for my suggestion, but glad they had enough sense to choose the right one. Money's suggestion was good, too, but I'm with Emilio. We need to include all of the African diaspora in the group's identity, not just people from the hood as we know it.

"Now that we have a name, let's define what the goals are," Mr. Adewale suggests, forcing us to think seriously about what we want to accomplish on our lunch break. He puts the mug back in its place and reclaims the legal pad I'm still quietly envying.

"I think it should center around surviving this place. South Bay is nothing like Westingle, man, for real." Nigel's right about that. His old school is very diverse. Rah still attends that school and receives most of the same educational and social perks that we do, while being closer to home. The students are bougie as all get out, but black is black and it's nice to be around our people on the regular.

"What do you mean by that?" Mr. Adewale asks, tapping his pen against the notepad in his hand.

"What I mean is that I can walk around my old campus and find us anywhere. Here, unless in the South Central clique, it's like we don't exist. And we never read black books in class either. My teachers at Westingle always taught with an Afrocentric twist."

"Well then, that's the first goal: to read more about black culture," Mr. A says, writing down the bullet points on the board. We all take notes like we're in class. Mr. Adewale inspires us to work when any other teacher would get the gas face for assigning more work outside of our required class reading. Ms. Toni walks into our meeting, ready to add some points of her own. I smile at my school mama, even though I think she's not pleased with me at the moment. It's admirable that she's taking on yet another club, with her already busy work schedule.

"Yeah, and black music should be on that goal list too, man. That shit's for real," KJ says, throwing his own spice into the mix. That's actually a good suggestion. If we keep the club up, we all might actually learn something.

"Okay, KJ, but can we hear suggestions without the profanity, please? There's a time and place for everything," Ms. Toni says, adding the mother balance we need to do this thing right. "We'll need to suggest officer appointments before taking our club request to the principal," she says, taking a seat at an empty desk next to Mr. A's.

"I think Jayd should be president, since it was her idea," Mickey says as she enters the meeting. My girl's right on time, and she's got my back without even knowing the full discussion. I wasn't going to say it, but that shit should be automatic. Nellie and Chance nod in agreement with Mickey and Nigel. Alia and Emilio also follow suit. Besides, I think I'd make a great president, but everyone doesn't seem to agree. I can already see opposition in my haters' faces.

"Uhm, no, I don't think so," Misty says, leading the hater coup. "This is a democratic society last time I checked, and we should vote about it like any other club." KJ strokes Misty's hand as she looks victoriously at our advisers. What kind of magic is she working on my former boyfriend?

"Can you even spell democratic?" Chance asks, making everyone laugh, except for Misty. Even KJ's whipped ass got a kick out of that one, but he quickly straightens up with a single disapproving look from Misty. Then she returns her attention to Chance.

"Can you spell black? Because if you could, you wouldn't be here right now." Everyone falls silent at the obvious truth: Chance and Alia are the only two white people present. Should I tell him that according to one of my dreams, he has just as much right to be here as anyone else? Maybe he already knows but is hiding it for some reason.

"This group is for anyone who wants to learn about black culture, not just students of African descent," Ms. Toni says. She's all about racial tolerance and preaches it every chance she gets.

"African descent? Who said anything about Africans?" Mickey asks. Like Nellie, she's clueless when it comes to our history and chooses to stay that way. For people like them, ignorance is bliss. I, on the other hand, have never had a choice about my knowledge. My ancestors made sure of that.

"We are from Africa, whether we claim it or not. Let's all agree on that fact right now, so that we never have to have this discussion again." With that one statement, Mr. Adewale sets the tone for the rest of the meeting.

"Now, back to business. We want to study black books, culture, and what else?" Ms. Toni asks, eyeing Mr. A's notes.

"The way we talk," Del adds. "And why ain't nobody as fresh as we is as Bow Wow would say." His crew laughs, more out of obligation than sincerity. It really wasn't that funny, and that song is so yesterday's news.

"And only Bow Wow can pull that line off and sound sexy," Mickey says. She loves her some Bow Wow. "You just sound ignorant when you say it," she adds, voicing my sentiments exactly.

"You're such a hater, Mickey," Misty says. Why is she talking when we both know she can't ever talk about anyone hating. It's her chosen career to be a professional hater. Hell, if hating was a sport, she'd be on the all-star team.

"Okay, back to the point," Ms. Toni says, her patience wearing thin. "Are there any other goals of the club we need to outline in our bylaws?"

"Man, why does it have to be so official? We're black. Can't we just have a chill club without all the rules and whatnot?" Money says. And by the grunts and nods in the room, I'd say he's voicing most of the other students' sentiments, but not mine.

"The reason it needs to be all official and whatnot is because we are black and our voices will never be heard if we don't go through the proper channels first," Mr. A says, looking at Ms. Toni, who vigorously nods in approval. As much as she's had to fight with these white folks up here over one thing or another, I know she's feeling the importance of this club.

"Exactly," Ms. Toni says. "And we want to be able to participate as a group in the next Cultural Awareness Festival since it's already the end of Black History Month. And in order to do that, we have to be on paper."

"Yeah, I agree," Emilio states. I don't know if he said that because he really feels that way or if it's because he's feeling me and wants me to be impressed with his little sophomore self. Either way it's working, because I'm feeling him more and more every day I see him.

"Nobody asked you. And what are you even doing here? You and the white boy," KJ says. And just like that, my pride in him has shifted to pure disdain.

"Okay, there's the bell for fifth period," Mr. Adewale says, rising from his desk. "We'll reconvene next week. Same time, same place." The other students say their good-byes and prepare for the last two periods of the day. Mickey, Nigel, and I step aside to quickly catch up, while Mr. A and Ms. Toni step outside to have a word before the next class arrives.

"So, what's the good word?" I ask my girl. Nigel steps behind his girlfriend and puts his arms around Mickey's growing waistline, holding her close for support. She doesn't seem too upset, so it can't be all that bad.

"Them fools said that I'm on academic probation or some shit, for the rest of the semester, saying my already marginal grades have fallen in the last few months." Mickey and Nigel rub her belly, loving their unborn child, and I'm glad for it because little Miss Thang can hear and feel everything in there. Those are part of the perks of being a caul baby like myself.

"I'm sorry, Mickey," I say, hugging her tightly and causing her to back up. I forget she's not one for affection unless it's coming from her man.

"Okay, shawty. It ain't that serious," she says, patting me on the shoulder like I'm a mere acquaintance and not one of her best friends.

"The hell it ain't," Nigel says, backing up from Mickey and looking at her over her shoulder. "If they kicked you out and made you go to the continuation school I would go crazy up in this place."

"Yeah, and the administration would love it if their star quarterback did some stupid shit like that," I say, laughing at my boy. But I know he's not joking.

"Well, I still have to bring my grades up by the end of the semester and keep a good attendance record if I want to stay at South Bay High School," she says, throwing her hands up and mocking a cheerleader.

"Then that's just what we're going to do, baby. From now on, you and I are study buddies." I don't know about that one. Nigel's serious about his education, but Mickey thinks of school as more of an annoyance than something she should take seriously.

"That sounds like a great idea," Mr. A says, interrupting our conversation. "But you're all going to be late if you don't sprint to class right now," he says, pointing at the wall clock. Ms. Toni walks in after him with a smile on her face.

"Ah, man, I can't get another tardy in math or my teacher's going to put me in detention," Nigel says, letting go of Mickey to grab his backpack and run for the door. As usual, Mickey couldn't care less about the time, and I'm not too worried because I'm heading to drama class. As long as I'm there within five minutes of the late bell, Mrs. Sinclair won't mark me tardy.

"Here's a hall pass just in case. But don't make it a habit," Mr. A says, passing us each a yellow slip with his signature on it. What a cool-ass teacher. Now I can take my time and go to the bathroom while I'm at it.

"Thanks, man. And for real, thank you for being our adviser," Nigel says, shaking Mr. Adewale's hand before he and Mickey exit ahead of me.

"Bye, y'all," I say to my friends. "And thanks again for the meeting," I say to Mr. Adewale and Ms. Toni, who look like they still have business to handle.

"You're welcome, Ms. Jackson," Mr. A says before focusing on Ms. Toni, who waves her good-bye.

The bathroom is calling me and the bell is ringing as I walk. Rather than try to make it to the bathroom in the drama room, I'll have to stop at the one in the main hall. I can't wait to tell Mama and Netta all about our first meeting of our new African Student Union. They're going to be so proud. With a new club to focus on, maybe the racist plays we choose in the drama club won't bother me so much. They can have their version of the story. With ASU, we'll tell our own version without apology, and I can't wait.

The line for the girls' restroom is always long after lunch, no matter which one we choose to use. It's like none of the girls want to interrupt their precious lunchtime to go pee before the warning bell rings, so we all end up standing in a long-ass line and running late to fifth period. The boys' restroom never has that problem. They go in and out ten times faster than we do. I usually go in the drama room because there's less competition down there. But today was just one of those days.

"Jayd, let me talk to you for a minute," Ms. Toni says, calling me out as I exit the girls' restroom. I knew this moment was coming, and I'm still not sure how I should react. If Ms. Toni were any other teacher, I wouldn't care too much what she thinks about me. But when Ms. Toni's mad at me I feel like I've disappointed my own mama.

"What's up, Ms. Toni?" I ask, repositioning my backpack on my back, ready for my hike down to the drama room. We haven't had a real conversation in a while. I know she has a ton of questions about my role in Laura's losing her voice on opening night of the last play we did. And I never had the chance to comment on her accusations about me having the hots for Mr. Adewale, but I hope she focuses on one issue at a time.

"Not here. Let's talk in my office," she says, leading me back down the main hall where her office is housed. She smiles to other students passing by and I follow, like a child waiting for her punishment. She unlocks the door to the ASB room and continues through the empty space to the back, where her headquarters are located. It's been too long since I've been back here. The stale smell of cigarettes mixed with her expensive, sweet-smelling perfume linger in the air. She must've gone off campus for a smoke break during lunch. Ms. Toni smells like home, and I've missed being in her presence.

"Have a seat, Jayd," she says, pointing to one of the two chairs by the door. She walks behind her crowded desk and sits across from me. The ASB students are out and about during fifth period, passing out flyers and making announcements in other classes, so we shouldn't have any interruptions for our impromptu counseling session.

"Nice plant," I say, noticing the orchids sitting on the corner bookshelf behind her desk. She looks like she's been reorganizing her crowded space. There are boxes of books and papers where stacks of the same used to be. Spring cleaning is a necessary chore for everyone, and I guess a person's workspace is no exception.

"Thank you. It was a gift from Laura and Reid," she says, smiling at the gift. "They wanted to show their appreciation for my help with *Macbeth*, even though Laura wasn't able to perform." I wish I had known that before. I would've reserved my compliment for something else not presented to her by the king and queen of evil. "Which brings me to why I want to talk to you. I won't keep you long. I know you're anxious to get to class."

The tardy bell for fifth period rings loudly in the quaint space. After the sound passes I remain quiet, waiting for the question I've been dreading.

"What really happened that night, Jayd? And don't tell me

you had nothing to do with it, because I don't believe that for a second." I look into Ms. Toni's bright eyes and notice two flecks outside of the brown pupils, similar to the ones present in my own. I can't lie to her, but I also can't tell her the truth. What do I do?

"You tell her what she needs to know, nothing more," my mom says, answering my thought with one of her own. *"I know you think she's one of us because she looks familiar, Jayd, and she may be. But all of us aren't always understanding, so be careful what you choose to reveal."*

"I know you're right, Mom. Thank you," I think back. Ms. Toni looks at me inquisitively, like Jeremy does when my mom drops in on my mind. I'd better say something so I can get out of here. Not that I'm in any rush to get to drama class, especially after what happened Monday. But I do want to get off of the witness stand.

"Ms. Toni, I can't explain what happened that night. All I know is that one minute Laura was harassing me and the next she couldn't speak." I readjust myself in the wooden chair and continue with my fiction. "I was just minding my own business, getting ready for the show."

"Minding your own business, huh?" Ms. Toni asks, unconvinced. She taps her long red fingernails on her desk, patiently awaiting the truth. But I can tell that her patience with me has just about run out.

"Yes. I was sitting at the vanity, doing my hair, when Laura started talking trash to me. I swear I didn't start the argument; she did. I know better than to strain my voice before curtain call." Ms. Toni smiles at me, but it's not a friendly one. What does she know that I'm not privy to? I feel like I'm being set up.

"Jayd, I've known you for over a year now, and if I know one thing about you, it's that you can't keep quiet when you feel threatened or slighted in the least bit. What Misty and

Laura did to you is reprehensible, but what you did was worse," she says, now tapping her desk with a pencil. "Do you want to know why?"

I'm not sure if Ms. Toni's question is rhetorical or if I should answer, so I'll just be quiet for now. It sounds like she's on my side, but not really.

"It's because I know you know better than to fight fire with fire. You're not petty, Jayd, and I expect more from you." My eyes begin to well up with tears. Ms. Toni's the only teacher at this godforsaken school who can make me cry. Hell, she's the only one who I'll let see me shed a tear.

"I was just defending my part," I say, without completely confessing my role in the twisted tale. If I tell her about how my dream of Laura snatching the crown off my head basically came true, she still wouldn't excuse my behavior. "With Misty's help, Laura stole my crown and I had to get it back."

"Not like that, you didn't." Ms. Toni puts down her pencil and rises from behind her desk. She's a good six feet tall, but today she looks much taller than usual. Or maybe I just feel smaller in her presence.

Without saying a word, Ms. Toni walks over to the bookshelf and scans her collection of titles. Last year I borrowed some great books from her and read them faster than any of the texts I read in my classes. Her selection constantly changes, and I love that. After careful consideration, she pulls one of the books off the shelf and thumbs through the pages as I await my sentencing. I wish I could share the tricks of our trade with Ms. Toni. I also want to get in that permed head of hers, but that's a conversation for another day.

"I want you to read this novel and let me know what you think of it," she says, walking around her desk and passing me the tattered book.

"*Voodoo Dreams*," I read aloud. I've heard of Jewell Parker Rhodes, but never read anything written by her. I have enough work to do with my AP exams coming up in a couple of months, not to mention the rest of the school and spirit work already on my shoulders. But from the way Ms. Toni crosses her thin arms across her chest, I don't think she cares about my personal dilemma right now. What she has made clear is that she knows Laura lost her voice opening night of the play because of something I did, whether she has proof, a confession, an eyewitness or not. And I can't continue telling Ms. Toni that her instincts are wrong when she obviously knows better.

"It's about a young girl reclaiming her African roots and the power that comes with that pride," she says, eyeing me carefully for a response, of which I give none. "It also shows what happens when you allow other people to dominate your psyche to the point where you get down to their level." Ms. Toni's dark brown eyes pierce mine. I can feel exactly what she's not saying, which is that I let Misty take my crown and went about getting it back in an underhanded way. I don't agree with her, especially when it comes to dealing with Misty, but I'll keep my opinion to myself.

"Sounds interesting. Thank you," I say, unsure of where this leaves the two of us. I hate it when she's mad at me. I feel like there's a heavy weight on my shoulders when Ms. Toni and I are at odds. But I hate it even more when Mama's on my case, which she would be if I ever confessed to a teacher that I used a potion on someone at school, no matter how cool I may think the teacher is. Mama would literally have my ass in a sling.

After a moment of silence, Ms. Toni takes a deep sigh and smiles at me as I read the introduction to my latest pleasure read. It's about my lineage, but fiction. It's not the first text I've ever read about my infamous great, great, great—and then some—grandmother, but this one looks hella juicy just from the opening lines. I can't wait to really get into it this weekend.

"You have to be responsible with your talents, Jayd. I know it seems as though I don't understand what you're going through, and that's why you turned to Mr. Adewale. But I know more than you think I do. I may not be a fine black man like Mr. A, as you call him, but give me some credit," she says, lightening the serious mood. "I've been here for you since last year, and I'm not planning on going anywhere." Now the tears are free-falling down my cheeks. I've missed my school mama.

"I know, Ms. Toni. I never meant to make you feel like I preferred talking to Mr. Adewale instead of you. It's just that our histories so are similar." Ms. Toni reaches over and pats my hand.

"I know. He filled me in on your commonalities," Ms. Toni says, choosing her words very carefully. "And I must say, I was surprised to know that he knew more about your family lineage than you've ever shared with me. But if you expect me to continue being on your side, you're going to have to let me in. We all have enemies in the administration and we have to stick together, capiche?" Ms. Toni says, sounding more like a mafia lord than a teacher. She stands up and opens her arms to let me in. I know we're cool now.

"Capiche," I respond, rising to accept her embrace. I've missed her hugs. I'll try not to do anything to ever get on her bad side again. "I'd better get to class now."

"Just remember what I said, Jayd. Your talents are nothing to be ashamed of, but be careful how you use them." I take my book and leave her office, ready to deal with the racist jerks in drama. Now that I've decided not to participate in the auditions for *The Crucible*, I have nothing but free time on my hands in class. And this novel is just the distraction I need to keep from cussing anyone out.

I didn't realize how tired I am until just now. I don't know if it was all of the arguing I did today or the emotional reunion me and Ms. Toni just had, but whatever it is has got me yawning all the way down the hill. I still have one more class to go after drama and work to do once I leave campus. I can't wait to get home, handle my business, and pass out for the night. We only have two more days of school before the weekend hits, and I'll be so happy when Friday finally does come, I probably won't know how to act.

~ 3 ~
Pride and Prejudice

*"We are the slave descendants of the African race/
Where proud is no disgrace."*

—THE ABYSSINIANS

As I walk into the empty space, I get the unfriendly feeling that I'm not alone. Dressed like a samurai warrior, I look around and scope the scene, waiting for my enemy to rear its ugly head. There are no windows or doors in the space and the walls are white, bare, and padded like in a mental institution. The bamboo floor crunches beneath my feet, making the only sound in the place as I walk around looking for an escape route. From the openness of the space and the way that I'm dressed, I think I'm in a dojo, and that's unfortunate because the only martial art I know is crazy. And we don't need a uniform for that kind of fighting in my hood.

Suddenly my opponents appear. The ceiling is open and it's again my fault that I didn't see my enemies coming: all I had to do was look up. One by one they fly in from outside and take shots at me. I should've paid more attention when my uncles and cousin watched Bruce Lee flicks on Sunday afternoons when I was younger. I have no idea what the hell to do. I duck from the first cloaked warrior, everything shrouded in black but its eyes. And then I realize that all I need to fight back is my sight: no karate shoes required.

"Call on your lineage, Jayd. Their eyes are yours," I hear my mom say from the walls of the room. I know I'm tripping if the walls are talking to me. But I have no time to worry about that right now. I have to fight back before I'm destroyed.

When the next fighter appears from the sky I look her dead in the eyes and don't back down. She tries to probe my thoughts, but I call on my lineage continually and rapidly, like I'm marathon praying, and my great-grandmother's powers come to my eyes. The warrior holds her head as I use Maman's powers to cause it to throb in pain with my look. When she can't take anymore, the warrior disappears the same way she appeared and the next contestant comes down to play.

"I won't be so easy to beat, little queen," he whispers in a low, guttural voice whose very tone catches me off guard. His first look knocks me down on the mat and I involuntarily bow at his feet. What the hell was that shit?

"Humble yourself, little one," he growls. Mama always taught me to salute my elders, but this fool ain't one of them, no matter how loudly he roars at me or how old he may be. I'll never bow to someone who's trying to kick my ass.

"My name isn't Leroy and you ain't Sho Nuff," I say, recalling a scene from one of my favorite movies, The Last Dragon. *"I only bow to elders who earn my respect." I jump up from the mat, possessed with a power I didn't know I had. My buoyancy precedes my understanding, but I'm rolling with it. I leap from one wall to the other without letting go of my opponent's gaze. This is some cool shit right here.*

Although there are no mirrors, I can see the reflection of my glowing eyes bounce off the white walls like Mama's do when she's on her game. My opponent smiles at my youth and that's his final mistake. Locking onto his gaze, I begin to see as he does, just like Mama can. Noticing the shift in power, his smile turns into a snarl and he begins to chase me around the dojo, matching me move for move. When he gets right behind me, I turn around and lock onto his gaze, my eyes now in full blaze. He sees his reflection through my vision and begins to break down under my sight.

With Mama's vision coming to the forefront, I'm using my enemy's power against him. I don't know much about martial arts, but isn't the first rule never to underestimate your opponent? I guess this fool missed that lesson.

"Bow to my lineage now, and I'll spare you your powers," I say, sounding more like one of my ancestors than myself. I look into his wet eyes and watch the tears fall down his covered face, moistening his mask. He struggles with the idea for a minute, but the longer he resists the more of his powers I strip away. I mentally continue to call my ancestors' names and those of other powerful ancestors in our lineage, including Netta's line. I don't know why people continually test us, when everyone knows how bad our house is. When will they learn not to mess with the Williams women?

"Challenges fortify us, Jayd. And when we stand up and face them—scared or not—we get stronger." My mom's right, because right now I feel invincible, even if it's only a dream.

"I pay homage to you, Queen Jayd, and to all of the queens before and after you," the man says, almost whispering, he's sobbing so hard. "Now get out of my head, please." My adversary's pleading softens my heart and my gaze. I didn't want to break him down and make him look like a punk. I just wanted him to leave me the hell alone.

"Ashe," I say, acknowledging the spiritual energy flowing through my veins. I soften my visual grip, but not before I catch my reflection staring back at me through his weakened eyes. I look like a straight-up warrior woman, remi-

*niscent of the pictures I've seen of our ancestor, Queen Calif***ʌ***.*
My samurai attire is gone and I'm now wearing a cutoff
skirt and sleeveless shirt, my tattoos and scars from battle
and other initiations prominently displayed. My most strik-
ing feature—other than my glowing eyes—is my crown.
Made of peacock feathers, it sits boldly on my head, similar
to the ones that the Native American dancers wore at the
school for last year's culture fest. What the hell?

"Jayd, wake up, girl. You're talking in your sleep again,"
Mama says, shaking me awake. Ever since my sleepwalking
incidents not too long ago, my grandmother has been more
watchful of me while I sleep. I look around our dark room
and come to, ready to talk about the experience I just had in
my spiritual dreamworld. But Mama quickly returns to her
bed to sleep. I guess I'll have to wait until daylight to get this
dream off my chest.

I'm so glad it's Friday I don't know what to do. This has
been one of the most challenging weeks I've had at South
Bay, and that's saying a lot, considering all of the drama I go
through around here on a regular basis. And today was no
exception. I turned in all of my Friday assignments and tried
to stay as quiet as possible in my classes for the entire day. It
worked well, but I'm sure I lost a few participation points
here and there, especially in English class.

Mrs. Malone didn't take too kindly to me bowing out of
our discussion on John Updike, which I was so passionate
about in Monday's class. But I said all I had to say for the
week about rich bitches thinking they own the world, including Charlotte, the one I sit across from in second period.
Mrs. Malone can read about the rest of my thoughts in my
paper abstract, which was also due today.

Mrs. Malone did bring up a valid point, which I may argue

with my pen instead of my mouth. Charlotte spoke again about the validity of dreaming and, as usual, she pointed to her daddy's work for evidence that dreams are the imagination's way of staying active while asleep. I damn sure wasn't going to admit out loud to finding any truth in her argument, but she did have a good point. My imagination gets quite a workout when I dream.

Since I awoke from my dream this morning, my sight has been tripping. I'm used to having very vivid dreams, of course. But being able to again see as Mama and Maman see, scared me a little. Being able to conjure the powers in my lineage was something I thought had been reserved for my forced dream-walk through Misty's mind on Valentine's Day. With Mama's help and my mom's guidance I was able to walk through Misty's dreams and undo all of her evil wishes. I unwove the twisted reality she created with the help of my ancestors and their collective vision powers, especially Maman's. But I don't think I'm supposed to be able to still use their powers, whether I'm dreaming about them or not. I'll have to ask Mama about that when I get to Netta's shop after school.

"Hey, Jayd. Got a minute?" Reid asks as I make my way up the steep hill to my sixth period gym class. Since dance was only offered for one semester, I was automatically enrolled in AP weight lifting, which is just fine with me. I like the solitude of working in the weight room. And I also like the tone I'm gaining in my arms and legs from the program I'm on.

"What is it, Reid? I don't have time to argue with you about anything right now," I pant. This hill is taking a lot out of me. I brought books for my English and government classes with me so I wouldn't have to go back to my locker after school. But now I'm seeing that that may not have been the best idea, with the sun beating down on me like it is. It's that time of year in Los Angeles, when it's cold in the morning and hot in the afternoon.

"I don't want to fight either. I just want to know what you're really up to," Reid says. I don't like the sound of his voice. He sounds a bit creepy, like a serial killer stalking his prey. And I'm in no mood to run, nor can I with my heavy backpack weighing me down.

"I have no idea what you're talking about." I look over my shoulder at Reid struggling to keep up with me. He's not fat, but he does have a spare tire or two hanging around his waist. If he didn't have money I doubt he'd have a girlfriend, especially one who thinks she's as pretty as Laura knows she is.

"Yes, you do. I know all about your little club," Reid says, this time even more disturbingly than before. "What do you think you'll accomplish with an African Student Union? And who do you think you are, bringing that type of club—if you can even call it that—to South Bay High?"

I halt my trek to look Reid in the eyes while I cuss him out. Who does he think he is, questioning me?

"Reid, in case you haven't noticed, I'm just as much a student here as you are. And because I attend this school, I'm allotted the same rights as everyone else, including you. So yes, I thought it would be a great idea if the students of African descent could have a club to call our own and represent our culture while we're at it. If you have a problem with that, tough." I spin back around on my heel and continue my walk toward the gymnasium, with Reid hot on my tail. What's gotten into him this afternoon?

"It will be tough for you and your new club. It won't last, Jayd. Mark my words. You will be defeated." And just like that, my eyes begin to glow like they did in my dream last night. The elder brother in the dream thought he could defeat me until I pulled on Maman's vision to help me kick his ass. And this time, without even calling on it, I can feel Maman's power resurface through my gaze. What the hell?

Noticing me stop, Reid walks around and looks at me, smiling like he's the victor, but he's in for a surprise. I look up, trying to gain control over my collective vision, but not before Reid looks directly into my eyes. And that's his final bad.

"My head!" Reid screams, putting his hands to his temples, trying to massage the pain away, like all the other victims that have fallen under the power of Maman's wrath. He looks a whole lot less bad when he's squirming. "What are you doing to me?"

"What am I doing to you?" I ask, now toying with him like the pest that he is. Reid needs to be humbled and I'm just the girl to do it. The bell must've rung a few minutes ago, because not a soul is present to witness their mighty ASB president fall to his knees at my feet. "You came up to me talking shit, or don't you remember? I was just trying to get to class." Maman's powers pulsate in my head. I can feel the blood pumping rapidly through my veins, the pulse matching the throbbing apparent in Reid's temples. This is the freshest shit ever.

"Jayd, stop. Whatever you're doing, please make it stop," Reid says, now quietly pleading. I can't help but feel sorry for him, but not that sorry. I still think he needs to learn a lesson in manners. But unfortunately I don't have the time to play with him any longer. We're given only ten minutes to dress out and then it's roll call. If I'm late I'll have to run a mile, and I'm not down for that, especially not in this heat.

"I don't take threats lightly, Mr. President," I say, almost whispering. "Remember that the next time you're feeling especially bold," I add, unlocking my visual hold on him. I have to get this power in check if I'm going to possess it on the regular.

Without making a sound, Reid makes his way up off the

ground and looks at me like he's just seen a ghost. I wish I could tell him how close to the truth that thought is, but that'd be taking it one step too far. He's already felt the power of my lineage and that's enough for now. Reid looks at me and I at him. It's about time he recognized there are other powerful people on this campus besides him. And, much like the fighters in my dream, the sooner Reid recognizes the powerful blood flowing through my veins, the better off he'll be.

When I finally made it to the weight room for sixth period, I worked out so hard I sweated out my press and curl, not that I mind much. Working out helps me calm down. That coupled with last night's psychic workout has given me a confidence I never knew I had. And after mentally kicking Reid's ass a couple of hours ago, I feel like I can conquer the world. I've been walking with this secret all day and I'm ready to let it out, but unfortunately today we have an audience at work.

I park my car in the crowded lot and make my way to the front door of Netta's Never Nappy Beauty Shop. The small salon is packed with clients, busy even for a Friday afternoon. Spring brings out the need to be beautiful in the sistahs and I'm looking forward to the tips. I ring the bell and look down at my buzzing phone, where Rah's name appears on the caller ID. The ladies in the shop all look up and wave at me without missing a beat from their vibrant gossiping.

I push the ignore button on my phone as Netta makes her way from the wash area to her station where the security buzzer is located. From the stressed look on my face, I know Netta can tell it's Rah I'm ignoring. It's only been a week since Sandy made her presence permanent at Rah's house, and I'm still feeling the impact of that atomic bomb.

"Hey, lil queen," Netta says, buzzing me through the front door. "Get your apron, girl, and get those two heads out of the wash bowls for me as soon as you wash up. And then I need you to get to work on the clients' boxes. We are way behind," Netta says, smiling and smacking her Doublemint chewing gum. She moves toward the dryers where all three seats are occupied and checks her clients' progress. The five women in the shop look at me as I cross the room to the wall where the closets are housed, momentarily suspending their chatter.

"Hi, y'all," I say, quickly following Netta's directions and heading to the back of the shop to cleanse my head and hands before I start my work. As usual, Mama's hard at work mixing products and tending to the heart and soul of Netta's Never Nappy Beauty Shop, like only she can.

"Well, well, well. Isn't it Miss Chatter-in-my-sleep," Mama says, kissing me as I greet her in the spirit room/office while she's working hard, as usual.

"Hi, Mama," I say, walking into the bathroom across the hall. I know she's about to grill me about last night, but we can't get into the ins and outs of my dreamworld while clients are present, even if we're in the back of the quaint building. I want to tell Mama so badly that I think I've maintained some of the gifts I received while sleepwalking last week, but this time they're positive and manageable—mainly because I'm staying in one place while dreaming instead of walking all over the place.

"So, how was your day?" Mama asks, mixing the sweet-smelling cream in her mortar, carefully adding ingredients as she blends. It smells like coconut and an herb I can't quite put my finger on. Whatever it is, the scent simultaneously lifts my spirits and calms me down.

"Let's just say I'm glad it's the weekend." And I'll be even happier when I get to my mom's house tonight. I want to take a long bath and finish the next chapter in my novel before I go to sleep. Ms. Toni was right; I'm loving this book.

"And yours?" I ask, retrieving the blend of Florida Water and lavender oil wash that we use to cleanse ourselves before working on clients' heads. I begin my wash, leaving the door open so I can hear Mama's response. I'm glad Netta has a bathroom for her clients in the wash area and a private one back here for us.

"It's going well," she says, glancing in the direction of the main shop. I know the women in there are haters of Mama's and they know better than to mess with her. I'm sure their energy must work Mama's nerves, even if she could crush them with one look. It must be hard, having all the power you need to hurt your enemies yet being wise enough to control it. That's one of many lessons that I've yet to master.

"Jayd, let's go," Netta yells. Mama smiles at me and passes me a clean towel from the shelf behind her to dry off from my quick cleansing.

"Thank you," I say, taking the towel from her hands. The scent of her work is on the towel, surging up my nose and through my entire body, making me feel better than I have all week. Mama smiles at my reaction and returns her focus to the creation in front of her. I finish patting myself dry and step back into the spirit room to return the cleansing potion to its place before I get to work.

When I walk back into the main room, the clients seated at the dryers stare toward the back of the shop where Mama's working and talk amongst themselves. At least they know better than to voice their gossip within our hearing, not that Mama cares one way or another. I can't wait until they leave so I can talk to her and Netta without spying ears and eyes, which won't be for a few more hours. But as long as we get some time together, I know I can get some clarity on my issues.

After the last client finally leaves, we get busy cleaning the shop and catching up on our days. I gather the wet towels and other laundry left behind from the busy day and put them in the laundry basket—I'll wash them first thing in the morning. After collecting the last of the dirty laundry, I replace all of the old linens with fresh ones and listen while Mama and Netta talk. They chat about the clients and their lives, but mostly about the progress of their individual hair regimens.

Like two doctors prescribing medicinal cocktails, Mama and Netta tailor each client's box with exactly what they need to maintain their healthy heads. It's amazing what you can learn about someone from how they wear their hair and what they use on it. Mama makes a product for everything from insomnia to being broke. I placed the cream Mama made earlier into small containers to spread out among the various clients in need of a calm head. No wonder I responded so well to the scent: at that moment it was just what I needed.

Last night's dream still has me a little shook up, not to mention the mental ass-whipping I gave Reid earlier this afternoon. The more time I've had to digest what went down today, the more certain I have become that I can never do that again, which means I have to learn how to control that part of my sight—just like I am doing with my dreams. What if someone had seen us? This time I would not have been able to feign innocence like I did when I choked up Reid's girlfriend. Laura would happily testify on his behalf and the witch hunt would be on—again. And I doubt that I could escape another accusation that I hurt a student with my voodoo ways. I'm sure the zero-tolerance rule applies to me using my gifts to do harm, too.

"You know Ms. Simms's husband is causing her all sorts of stress. Did you see those bald patches popping up all over her scalp? She's going to need some of your quick-grow balm with honey, Lynn Mae. A lot of it," Netta says, picking through the various containers of Mama's creations on the counter across from the cabinets where the clients' boxes and other storage items are housed. It takes up an entire wall and is organized to perfection. Netta's a true professional about her shit.

"And some of the aloe vera cream we made last week. That'll help those scratches on her head heal faster. She needs to stop letting that man and his gambling stress her out. He's been that way since I went to that church, and ain't changed in the thirty years since," Mama says, passing her a small jar full of her suggestion. Netta takes it from her and places it into the plastic box.

"Well, you know that woman as well as I do. She thinks as long as he shows up at church on Sunday morning that there's a chance her husband can be saved," Netta says, sealing the box and moving on to the next. They have about ten more to go before they're done with that project and on to the next. There's always something to do around here.

"That's the problem right there," Mama says, shaking her hand up in the air. "These folks think it's up to someone else to save a grown-ass person. The only way someone can truly be saved is to do the work themselves. That's where the healing begins." Netta nods her head vigorously in agreement while scanning the remaining inventory.

"And if you try to do it the other way around, you end up losing your hair and coming to us to help save you," Netta says, making us all laugh. These are the most healing times we have together; just talking and cleaning. I could use a little therapeutic conversation of my own, but I'll ease my dream and daily events into the conversation at the right time. Right now I'm enjoying the two elders in the room vibing with one another.

"That's why she wants you to come speak at the church tomorrow. She and all of them other women up there want the chance to pick your brain about saving their marriages," Netta says, causing Mama to roll her eyes.

"Mama, you're going to church in the morning?" I ask, completely shocked at the thought of Mama sitting quietly through one of Daddy's sermons. I thought I'd never see that happen in my lifetime.

"Hell no," Mama says, equally shocked at me for even having the thought in my head. "Every year for Black History Month, colored folk month, African American month, or whatever the hell else they call the shortest month of the year, these fools at your granddaddy's church ask me to come and do a talk about traditional African culture, like they don't remember that we have a shared history of being the survivors of captivity in this country." Mama sucks her teeth out of disgust at the thought of stepping foot in Daddy's church.

"I hear you, Lynn Mae," Netta says in agreement, without looking up from her work. Netta always has Mama's back, no matter what the issue is.

"Some people are so ashamed of their African heritage that they'd rather pay someone to come and talk about our collective history than do the digging themselves. Some black people are simply uncomfortable with the idea of being African," Mama says with a stressed look across her brow. She really needs to relax. A vacation would do Mama some good.

"Tell me about it," I say, easing into my confession for the day. "This white boy at school who thinks he owns the place is mad at me because I initiated the first African Student Union on campus. He actually had the nerve to step to me today and warn me about what would happen if I didn't back down from making the club official." Mama and Netta stop their organizing and look up at me, smiling.

"Good for you, little Jayd. She's sporting her crown high

on her head, ain't she, Lynn Mae?" Netta says, beaming from ear to ear. I knew they'd be proud of me if I eased my story in at an opportune moment.

"Good for you, Jayd," Mama says, returning to her duties. "And don't worry about that white boy. They're always threatened by the presence of a strong black woman," she says, and I know Mama knows all about that kind of drama. "I decided a long time ago that I'm not here to make anyone comfortable, especially not white men. As far as I'm concerned, this is their country and they tend to think that this is their world, too."

"Amen to that," Netta chimes in. The two of them together crack me up every time, except for when they're mad at me. I just hope this evening is not one of those times after I tell them how I reacted to Reid's racist threat, even if I am slightly proud of my newfound clout.

"Even some of the black folks at the school are hating," I say, grabbing the broom and dustpan from the corner in preparation for my next chore. "And the majority of the ones that are participating in the club don't want to take the time to learn anything other than what they already think they know about being black. But luckily Mr. Adewale and Ms. Toni are our advisers, and I know they'll make sure we receive the proper guidance." I'm looking forward to spending some time with both of my favorite teachers outside of our regular classes.

"Of course the black students are hating," Netta says, now prepping fresh tools for tomorrow while Mama finishes the clients' boxes. If Friday was this busy, tomorrow should be off the chain—and so will the money we earn.

"Jayd, you'll soon learn that sometimes the very people who need light the most will be the ones who want it the least," Mama says while I continue sweeping. There's more hair on this floor than in a horse's mane. Any other beauty shop would simply throw it away, leaving the clients' heads vulnerable to all kinds of curses and other negative things. But Mama and Netta take special precautions to make sure that their clients' hair is disposed of in the proper, spiritual way it deserves.

"I had a best friend once who thought I was too black for my own good. She was black too, but not in culture. I knew some white folks that were more black than that girl was," Netta says, checking her station's inventory one more time before shutting the lights off in that section. "I never could understand why some black folks get pissed when whites want to join the religion, sing our songs, eat our food—not that we let them in, but I can understand the desire. Being black is where it's at for me."

"But everyone doesn't share that frame of mind," Mama interjects, smiling at her best friend. "Different people's relationship to the culture is personal, and you must respect their frame of reference, too. In this life, all roads are valid," Mama says, closing all the boxes before returning them to their cabinets. "And I've ceased caring about what white folks think about my way of life. Why the hell should I bite my tongue to please them when they couldn't care less about my feelings, or my ancestors' for that matter?" Mama looks at me and knows something else is on my mind. Now is as good a time as any to lay it all out on the table.

"I feel the same way, Mama, and showed Reid exactly how I felt about him threatening me," I say. Mama stands at full attention and puts her right hand on her hip, giving me a look that tells me to continue with the entire story. "Last night my dream was about me fighting off my enemies with our ancestors' powers and yours too," I say, continuing with my work while coming clean. Mama and Netta are silent, taking it all in. "And today I was able to use Maman's powers on Reid. It was so cool," I say, sounding like an excited schoolgirl who just learned a new double Dutch move. I wish life were that simple.

"You did what?" Mama asks. She and Netta are both now staring at me in disbelief, but I think they're still a little proud of my spiritual development.

"Oshune be praised," Netta says, dramatically raising her hands to her mouth as she salutes our mother orisha.

"Netta, not now," Mama says, cutting her eyes at Netta, who immediately busies herself with shutting down the rest of the shop. It's time for all of us to go. But from the way Mama's green eyes are glowing, I don't think she's finished with me quite yet.

"Jayd, I'm glad that your dreams are becoming more powerful and that you're excited about this recent development, but you can't use your gift of sight like that, especially not at school, girl." I knew Mama would feel this way. I should've kept it to myself for a little while longer, at least until after we got the African Student Union officially recognized as a legitimate club by South Bay High's administration.

"But what if I get attacked again? Reid really feels threatened by me and so does Laura." I also just like having the power on hand to cripple their conceited asses when they get carried away, but I'll leave that part out.

"And rightfully so. That girl tried to steal your crown and you got it back, just like any other Williams woman would do," Netta says, glancing sideways at Mama while collecting the trash bags to dump once we're outside. Her husband should be here any minute to pick her and Mama up.

"Netta, stop encouraging her," Mama says, snapping at her homegirl, but with nothing but love in her voice. "The girl's got too much power and you know it." Mama walks over to the sink and washes her hands. Her salt-and-pepper hair gently bounces off her shoulders as her shapely frame seemingly glides across the hardwood floor. Mama looks like she could be my mom's older sister more than the mother of eight grown kids.

"Yes, but so do you. Isn't this what we've been praying for?" Netta says, not backing down from her stance, no matter what Mama says. Netta always has my back in situations like these because she thinks I'm going to make a great voodoo queen one day, just like Mama is. I don't think anyone can be as bad as Mama, but if I can call on her powers when I need to, that would make me almost as gangster with my sight as she is with hers. And I'll take whatever I can get, even if it's only temporary.

"Jayd, I'm glad the ancestors have blessed you with the ability to bring some of the things that occur in your dream-world back with you when you wake up, but this is one gift you're not ready to receive." Mama walks over to where I'm standing and hugs me tightly. My head melts into the softness of her body and I let a few tears fall within her sweet embrace. I knew she was going to make me give it back, and I know she's right. I can see myself abusing the gifts of my lineage, and that's not what they're here for, no matter how flyy I feel.

"Well, what do I do when Reid threatens me again?" I ask while wiping my face dry. "You should've seen the look on his face before his head started to throb. He was so smug about shutting down the club. I know he won't quit until I lose." Mama strokes my ponytail. I forgot how good it feels to have someone besides me playing in my hair.

"Some people need to grow up, plain and simple," Netta says, putting extra combs in the cleansing solution near the wash bowls before moving on to the brushes and the rollers now that she's completed all of the mandatory nightly duties. We can never be too prepared. "And then there are those who refuse to leave their comfort zone and feel they never have to grow. That's a very privileged perspective that we as black women have never had the luxury of knowing."

I know that's right. South Bay High is full of the privileged and comfortable. And Netta's right about them wanting to stay that way. They never leave their beautiful beach areas to deal with our reality, while we're supposed to willingly as-similate to theirs. *Whatever* is what I say to that idea.

"And you, little girl, have to know when to stop. You have more knowledge than some people will ever have, and that can be a disadvantage as much as it is an advantage. You have to learn when to talk and when to listen. Humbling yourself will be difficult, especially with your crown. But it's neces-sary for survival, and you are living for more than yourself. Remember that and your head will never overheat again," Mama says, feeling my forehead as if I have a temperature and her hand is the thermometer.

"Yes, ma'am," I say, looking up into Mama's eyes through my watery vision. I can already feel the gift leaving my eyes the longer Mama looks at me. She takes her hand off my fore-head and looks at Netta watching us. Netta shakes her head from side to side and lets out a deep sigh, knowing Mama's already started to strip my new powers away.

"It's time for your remedy, little girl. And with that wild dream you had last night, I'd say the sooner we suppress your premature powers the better," Mama says, indicating to Netta that she needs her assistance.

"But Mama, I love this newfound road of walking in my ancestors' shoes. It feels empowering. Do we have to wash all of the sight away?" I plead, unwillingly following Mama and Netta to the shrine room. I don't want to give my powers back. I'm just getting used to them.

"We have to. The things you can do in your dreams are out of order with your life experience and wisdom. Too much power too early can be very destructive," Mama says. Netta lets out a final sigh of disapproval before turning on the lights in the back room.

"Okay, if you say so. But I think the ancestors' teasing me with this has been a cruel and unusual punishment. I think I should be able to keep a little souvenir, given all of the drama we just went through." Mama looks at me and smiles like she knows something I don't.

"Consider your memory a souvenir, Jayd. Now let's get moving. I've got work to do at home and so do you when you get back to your mother's apartment. You also need to write this entire experience down in the spirit book." Mama follows Netta to the shrine and instructs me to kneel on the mat while they pray.

While kneeling in front of Netta's shrine, the black velvet painting of a woman kneeling at a river begins to glow. The picture changes every time we're at the shrine. Once finished, Netta pulls a small, blue cloth bag from the top shelf of the shrine and hands it to Mama. Mama gives me the bag of herbs and instructions for taking the bath once I get back to Inglewood. Netta then hands Mama a red envelope.

"You're going to dissolve a teaspoon of these herbs from the red pouch in a glass full of water and swallow swiftly. Don't think about the heat as it goes down," Mama says, handing the red envelope to me. "Once you're done bathing with the mixture in the blue pouch, gather the herbs with a strainer and put them in a plastic bag," Mama continues, grabbing her purse and shawl from the coatrack behind the door upon hearing Netta's husband honk their truck's horn. Netta does the same thing and turns off the lights as we each head to the front of the shop where my car is parked. "Bring them to me in the morning. And don't forget to take the entire dose, Jayd. We can't take any chances."

"You have no idea how powerful your bloodline is, little

Jayd," Netta adds. Mama looks back at her friend, who promptly shoos her out of the front door so she can set the alarm. Mama hates for Netta to brag about our lineage, but she and I both know that Netta's telling the truth. Mama doesn't like to act too proud, mainly because she says that it incites jealousy in other people. And jealousy can make people do some crazy things. We can all testify to that.

~ 4 ~
So Fine, So Furious

"I hate you so much right now."

—KELIS

When I finally arrived at my mom's apartment last night, I was so tired that all I could do was take my prescribed bath and go straight to bed. I took the entire portion of the dried herbs in water and collected my bath herbs for Mama to throw away. I didn't recognize all of the ingredients, but guinea peppers and cayenne were two of the strongest peppers in the red envelope. The mixture was so spicy I could swear that my blood was boiling. I got so hot in my sleep that I sweated out two nightgowns and the sheets on the small couch that doubles as my bed on the weekends.

I wish I could've kept the use of my other powers. That was the coldest shit ever. But like Mama said last night, I have to master my own gift of sight before I can use anyone else's effectively. It's still nice to know that my ancestors have my back when I do need them and that a large part of my powers—once I mature a bit more—will be to call on my ancestors and elders in my dreams when need be.

I don't remember my dream last night, but I can tell that my sight is back to normal, whatever that means. Thank God I got some good sleep last night, and because it was uninterrupted, I'm ready to start my Saturday off right, even if it is too early to be up and out on the weekend. I have to stop at

Mama's house before I go to work, which means I had to get up extra early this morning. Hopefully everything worked according to Mama's plan so we can leave the shop early this evening, leaving me with some time to chill this weekend. We should have a shop full of heads today and I'm anxious to get started.

When I get downstairs to my mom's car I notice a note stuck inside the windshield wipers. I free the paper from the glass and get in the car to warm her up, tossing the letter into the passenger seat without opening it: I already know it's from Rah. It takes a good five minutes before I feel like everything's flowing just right in the eleven-year-old vehicle before I put her into first gear. There's still a lot of zoom in my mom's compact Mazda, but it takes a minute to get there.

I put my headphones in my ears after making myself comfortable in the driver's seat. Pulling the zipper closed, I place my Lucky Brand bag on the passenger's seat and flip through my playlist for the perfect morning soundtrack. My iPod's the only sound I've got in this little car and I'm not complaining. Whether the music's coming out of the speakers in the car or the travel ones in the passenger's seat, it makes the half-hour drive to Compton more enjoyable.

Before I pull out of the parking lot and onto my mom's street and head toward Mama's house, my cell rings with Kelis's lyrics announcing my first call of the day. I reassigned an oldie but goody ringtone to Rah, since he's always coming back with the same bull year after year. I push the ignore button without guilt and keep it moving. He promptly sends me a text message asking if I got the note. Is he watching my every move now or what? If he keeps it up, I'm going to have to get a restraining order to keep his stalking at bay. When Rah starts tripping like this, I know he's feeling like shit—as he should.

I can't believe Rah and I are fighting again over Sandy's

trifling ass. Sandy suckered him for the umpteenth time and the more and more I think about it, the less sympathetic I become. I admit I've felt like crap ever since last Saturday, when I found out about Sandy and Rahima moving in with Rah while she's on probation. I miss him as I always do when we're not talking. But then I think about the unfair exchange rate ever present in our relationship—which is usually to his benefit—and I get even hotter. How could he do this shit to me—again? How could he do this to us?

After a smooth drive through the various hoods between Inglewood and Compton, I arrive at Mama's house. It's only seven in the morning and that means most of the neighbors are still asleep, except for a few elders outside enjoying the morning air. Mr. Gatlin—our asshole of a neighbor across the street—is watering his lawn. He's so meticulous about his property that he calls the police on anyone who sets foot on his lawn. Why doesn't he just fence himself in? That'll save us from having to deal with his crazy ass and protect his precious grass. Sounds like a win/win situation to me.

After parking the car at the house across the street to our left—two houses down from Mr. Gatlin—I walk over to Mama's house and open the back gate.

"Hey, girl." I greet Lexi, Mama's guard dog, and follow her back to the spirit room where I can hear Mama already working. Usually she's opening the shop with Netta by now. But this morning we're going to be a little late.

"Good morning," I say before opening the screen door to the little house attached to the back of the garage. The smell of maple syrup and molasses lingers in the air, causing my stomach to growl. My mouth was so hot this morning from last night's concoction that I forgot all about eating breakfast.

"Are you hungry, baby?" Mama says, directing me to sit at the kitchen table where a piping hot bowl of oatmeal is waiting. How did she know I'd be hungry? I take my seat, placing my purse and the bag of herbs from my bath in the center of the table.

"Yes, thank you," I say, claiming the spoon sitting to the right of the bowl and digging into the hot cereal. Mama gives me a kiss on my cheek and takes the plastic bag full of wet herbs to where the shrines are housed on the other side of the small kitchen. There isn't much space in here, but it's enough to get our work done and that's all that matters. Sitting right outside the door, Lexi barks at the sound of our next-door neighbor—and Mama's biggest hater—Esmeralda's back door opening and shutting. She must be letting her three fat cats out for the day. She's been pretty quiet since Mama kicked her ass in the spirit realm last week, but we'll see how long that'll last. Esmeralda's always up to no good, and Mama's keenly aware of that unavoidable fact of life.

"What is this I see? You don't come home to me. When you don't come home to me I can't deal, can't bear." I reach into my open bag and grab my cell, silencing Rah's call again. Why is he jocking so hard this morning?

"Problems with Rah?" Mama asks from her kneeling position on the bamboo mat. The white candles provide a warm glow in the room this morning, along with the bright sunrise gleaming through the windows. I can't help but feel calm when in the spirit room.

"How did you know?" I ask, finishing the last spoonful of the sweet cereal. Damn, that was good. Ironically, she and my dad make the best oatmeal I've ever tasted. Even if Mama can't stand him, I'm glad they have that skill in common.

"Girl, please," Mama says, now emptying the contents of my small baggie onto the mat with her cowrie shells and other tools for divination. "Any song with such strong lyrics belongs to that boy." She looks up at me and signals me to join her on the mat now that I'm done eating.

"I'm still in shock over him and Sandy shacking up," I say,

kneeling next to Mama. She looks me in the eye, checking for herself to see how I'm doing. Without another word, Mama takes one of several glasses of water from the ancestor shrine and begins pouring the libation, beginning the reading. Because we have to get going sooner than later, Mama performs an abbreviated version of her regular prayers and asks for direction on how to dispose of my medicinal bath herbs, now that we've suspended my extra powers for the time being.

"Ashe Oshe," Mama says, calling out the name of the odu— or spiritual story—that accompanies the five cowries facing up on the mat. Each combination of the sixteen flattened shells has a story and name behind it. And in this case, the odu Oshe, which belongs to our mother Oshune and father Legba, comes up and that's a very good sign.

"Ashe," I say, acknowledging the odu as well. Mama throws the four coconut pieces known as obi, which are also housed on the ancestor shrine, and asks for a simple yes or no answer so we can close the reading and get to work. But the answer is a solid no, indicating that an offering has to be made before we can leave.

"Jayd, have you been truthful in your association with the boys in your life?" Mama asks, obviously seeing the same thing I do. "Oshe deals with all of the sweet things in creation, but it also warns against jealousy and rivalry," she says, now asking the ancestors and orisha what exactly they want us to do.

"Yes. It's they who haven't been truthful with me," I say, watching as Mama recasts the obi. I can remember playing with the shells when I was a little girl and how much fun it was. I like divining because it reminds me of a math game. But I can't officially cast the shells until after my formal initiation into the priesthood, which is coming up soon.

"Dada ni," Mama says, reading the "yes" and quickly putting up the cowries and obi. "You need to make sure you tell the truth when dealing with your friends, both male and female.

Someone around you is jealous of your blessings in more ways than one. And when it comes down to it, the person in the right also walks with truth, Jayd. Always make sure you're on the right side."

"Will do," I say, studying the seriousness in Mama's eyes. There's more she's not telling me, but I'm sure I know all I need to for right now. Mama rises from the mat, collecting the herbs used in the reading and tosses them into the small garbage can in the corner. She then ties the white trash bag and pulls it out of the can, handing it to me. I get up and claim the bag.

"Put this at the curb for trash collection and don't look back at it once you walk away. Once you've finished you can go on to the shop. Tell Netta I'm right behind you," she says, kissing me on the cheek and turning me toward the door.

"Okay. I'll see you in a few," I say, grabbing my purse off the table. I knew Mama wasn't going to ride to work with me, even though we are going to the same place. I know she likes to walk, but it's just quicker to get there by car. She's not comfortable with the idea of me driving her around, but hopefully one day she'll trust me enough to give her a lift.

"And we have an errand to run after work. So don't make any plans," Mama says to my back as I head out of the spirit room. Damn, and I was hoping to end our workday early, or at least my part of it. All work and no play makes Jayd a dull and sour sistah. But this is no time to argue. By the end of our busy day, I hope Mama will be just as tired as I know I'll be, and we can put off our errand until another day.

I dispose of the trash bag as instructed and head to my mom's car parked across the street. To avoid looking at the trash on the curb I turn my head back toward the house and notice that my grandfather already has a visitor on the porch early this Saturday morning. Maybe she's a Jehovah's Witness coming to spread the love. When I get to my mom's ride I

can hear the lady's voice getting louder as Daddy comes out
on the porch to talk with her. Something about her body language tells me she's not here to spread the good word.

"I will have you for myself, Pastor James. The Lord's way is
more powerful than any heathen's witchcraft," she says, shaking she's so upset. I look more closely and recognize the
woman from the fight she and Mama had when she thought
it would be a good idea to drop a cake off for Daddy one day.
I thought she'd learned her lesson when Mama went off on
her that time, but I guess not. Daddy probably thinks Mama's
already at Netta's, or I doubt he'd be entertaining that crazy
broad on the front porch where everyone can see his business so clearly.

"Not here," Daddy says, pointing for the lady to leave, but
she's not budging. It looks like she's brought something with
her that she's trying to give to him, but he won't accept her
gift, which only pisses her off more.

"You're a man of the cloth," the woman says, almost yelling.
"You don't have to be afraid of your wife. God will protect
those who do his will." Daddy looks down at the woman like
she's lost her mind. Even Daddy knows Mama's gods are just
as powerful as his own. And because he knows that, he tries
to get the woman to leave before she has to learn that lesson
the hard way, since she obviously didn't get it the first time
around.

I feel obligated to help Daddy because this chick is ready
to show her entire ass, and I don't want Mama to hear this
bull. I unlock the car door with my mom's key instead of the
remote, setting off the alarm and drawing their attention to me.

"Hey, Daddy," I say, waving at him after pressing the alarm
key and silencing the loud noise. Car alarms go off all the
time around here, so that's nothing unusual. Hopefully I didn't
wake up anyone who's still sleeping. Daddy looks both grateful and embarrassed that I'm here. But less than a second

later his face turns gray as he realizes that if I'm here on the weekend, Mama must not be far behind.

Seeing the look in my grandfather's eyes, the lady looks past him and into the house, expecting to see my grandmother appear. When nothing happens, the lady looks across the street at me and then at my grandfather. She takes a step forward and forces whatever's in her hand into his right palm.

"She can't hurt you anymore, Pastor James. When you're ready, I'm here waiting on you," she says before turning around and walking down the porch steps to her car, parked in front of Esmeralda's house. I think that's more than a coincidence, but I'll worry about that later. Daddy walks down the steps and across the yard to where I'm still standing. We both watch her pull off, grateful she left before Mama came out. That would have been a tragedy for all of us.

"Good morning, Tweet," Daddy says nervously, bending down to give me a hug. "So, what did you hear?" he asks, looking down at me and waiting for the playback.

"Not much, but enough to know that woman's crazy," I say, leaning up against the car while Daddy does the same. He looks almost as tired as Mama does after she pulls an all-night work session. Satisfied with my response for the moment, Daddy stands up straight and I get into the car and sit in the driver's seat, ready to finally get to work. It's a few minutes to eight and I know that some of the regular customers have already arrived at Netta's salon, which means my money's also there waiting for me.

"What are you doing here so early anyway? Shouldn't you be at work?" he asks, looking at Mr. Gatlin a couple of houses down. I know he heard everything I did, and probably more.

"Me and Mama had something to do first," I say, starting the car. Daddy looks down at me and closes my door while I fasten the seat belt across my body. A girl can never be too careful.

"You should come visit the church again, Jayd. I think you have a lot of talent, especially with the way you handled yourself at the memorial service," Daddy says, reminding me of Tre's death. "You might even want to consider giving a speech on Easter Sunday a few weeks from now. It happens to fall on youth Sunday this year, and we're letting the young people take it over." I wonder if that's because all of the adults are too busy sinning.

"I'll think about it," I say. "But right now I have to get to work." Daddy smiles at me before walking back across the street and letting me go. Through my rearview mirror, I can see him looking toward the backyard. I can't read his mind, but if I could I'd bet he's counting his blessings for Mama not coming out of the backhouse—where the spirit room is housed—while his side trick was there.

I will never understand why Daddy cheats on Mama or why Mama has stayed married to Daddy all of these years, knowing how he rolls. But there are a lot of things Mama does that I don't fully understand, nor do I try to anymore. I just do what I'm told and trust her—period. The rest of it, as Mama says, is grown folks business and I'm not that grown yet. Being the youngest in Netta's shop reminds me of that every time I'm at work. And today will be no exception.

Just as I expected, the shop was full all day long. We barely got a lunch break, taking ten minutes here and there to nibble on the food Mama or Netta brings for our long workdays every weekend. Now that the day is almost over, all except for one of the clients is done for the day. Netta had to do some serious heat repair for this sistah's hair. She went to another stylist while out of town and the lady jacked her up. The sistah cried through the entire story and vowed to never let another beautician touch her head—ever.

"Come on, Jayd. We have to go shopping for spirit supplies. There's a lot of work to be done and I need to stock up," Mama says, hanging her work apron on the hook next to the lockers. Is she serious? It's almost seven and any botanica we go to is going to be at least a half hour away. By the time we're done it'll be after nine, leaving me hardly any time to myself this evening. What the hell?

"Mama, can't we go tomorrow? It's late and I'm tired," I whine, following Mama's lead and getting ready to go, even though I hope we're going in two different directions. Netta's in the back on the phone with her husband, making big plans to go stepping tonight. Netta loves to dance and bowl almost as much as she likes doing hair. And with Sundays being her slowest day, there's no need to worry about coming in early tomorrow. I rarely work Sundays because there's so little to do. And I think Netta likes having her shop to herself for one day a week.

"No, we can't, Jayd, and stop whining. Botanicas are closed on Sundays because most of the owners and practitioners still attend Sunday mass," Mama says, grabbing her large overstuffed hobo bag from the coatrack and opening the front door of Netta's shop. It was a warm day and it's still a nice evening. The sun hasn't completely set, leaving an orange hue across the darkening blue sky. Today would have been a perfect beach day and I know my friends both in the hood and in the South Bay took advantage of the gift.

Netta comes to the front of the shop and waves at us without pausing her phone conversation. She's got the truck today and as soon as she's done here, she'll go home and pick up her man. I'm glad someone's relationship seems to be working out.

"See you tomorrow and odabo," Mama says, waving goodbye to her best friend. Even if they don't know the language that well, they still speak Yoruba every chance they get, especially when greeting each other. Mama says it's important to speak whatever African language you know, to retain the tongue and the memory that intrinsically comes along with it. We pray and sing in Yoruba, too, for the same reason.

"Odabo and be safe, sis. See you Monday, lil Miss Jayd," Netta responds, returning to her office before I can say goodbye. Whatever stepping competition they've got going on tonight must be fierce. Netta's hella fit for a woman in her thirties, let alone her fifties. She stays on her feet and that keeps her looking young, just like Mama.

"We're going to The Path off Broadway and Main," Mama says. That's her favorite botanica and is owned by a friend of hers. Mama stops outside the front door and gives some coins to the Legba shrine for the shop. "You're driving." Mama walks to the passenger's side of my mom's car and waits for me to unlock the doors. Astonished, I clumsily look for the keys in my purse, which are buried at the bottom of the damned thing. That's the problem with upgrading the size of a purse: no matter how big it is, you can always fill it up with junk.

"I'm sorry. I know they're here somewhere," I say, frantically searching through old receipts, hall passes, and candy wrappers. Why do I need all of this garbage hanging off my shoulder? I'm going to have to see about downsizing my summer handbag. This is too much for a sistah to go through every time I need something.

"Part of being a responsible driver is knowing where your keys are at all times," Mama says, rolling her eyes at me impatiently.

"Here they are," I say, proudly pointing the remote at the car and unlocking the doors. For the first time, Mama's getting in the car with me behind the wheel. I just hope we make it to our destination in one piece or I'll never hear the end of it.

*   *   *

When we finally arrive at the store, the parking lot is packed with people coming and going. It doesn't help that there's a Taco Bell right next door, sharing the tiny lot with the spiritual supply megastore. We find a parking space at the very back of the store and claim it quickly before someone else does.

"Here, Jayd, you push the basket. We have to stock up," Mama says, walking down the wide aisles of the warehouse. There are several botanicas Mama likes to patronize, but this one is by far her favorite.

Each aisle is color coded according to the orisha it represents, offering incense, candles, cloths, sacred objects, and anything else needed to get the work done. The owner even made sure to group the orishas according to personality and preference. Oshune is on the same aisles as Yemoja and Olokun. Ochosi, Ogun, and Legba are together while Sango is on the same aisles as Oya, Oba, and Orunmilla. Obatala and the ancestors are located on the two middles aisles between the other orishas. Then there's an aisle at the very front of the store, next to the cashiers for other deities who are not as well known.

"Alaafia, Queen Jayd!" the owner, Miguel, says to me, then also greets my grandmother in Yoruba. Bowing and blowing kisses to her as he walks toward us, down the aisle for Oshune, he smiles and looks around to make sure no one sees him. Mama hates an audience, even if her crown makes it impossible for her to walk around unnoticed in the voodoo community.

"Alaafia, Miguel. *Cómo estás?*" Mama replies, gently tapping his shoulders, indicating he may rise and give her a hug. Miguel is one of Mama's oldest initiates into the religion. I'm ever amazed at Mama's connections in various hoods.

"*Muy bien. Y tú? Tu familia es bien, sí?*" His Spanish accent makes the words roll right off his tongue, much like when

Emilio and Maggie speak in their native language. But their accents are different, making their dialects sound like a different language to me, even though I know they're all speaking Spanish.

"Sí, mi familia es bien, gracias," Mama says, her Spanish perfect but without the accent. Mama speaks a little bit of the various languages that come with the devotees in the religion. She can converse in multiple Creole languages and Portuguese, too, which always trips me out. I hope to inherit Mama's talent for picking up different words here and there.

"And little Jayd. You're looking especially lovely this afternoon in your Yeye's favorite color, yellow," he says, complimenting my mother Orisha before crossing both arms across his chest and slightly bending his right knee before hugging me tightly. He does this to honor my lineage even though I'm not initiated yet. Nor am I his elder, so a bow would be inappropriate. I love the reverence and respect I receive when I'm around Mama because I am her grandchild. If I'm going to be a part of any clique to get props, it's got to be Mama's crew.

"Gracias, Señor Miguel." He's got to be at least Mama's age, but I can never tell how old my elders are in our community. Most of them appear to be ageless. They seem to stop aging around fifty or so years. On the other hand, the elder sisters and brothers at Daddy's church seem to age more rapidly.

"Can I help you find anything, Iyalosha?" he asks Mama while escorting us farther down the aisle. Mama checks her list and begins reading it off to Miguel. I'm glad he's here. His assistance will make the shopping go by faster and with little effort from me. I want to get back to my mom's apartment, watch reruns of *The Game* and finish reading another chapter or two in my novel. I'm about halfway through the text and it's really getting good.

I follow Miguel as he moves expertly through Mama's list, organizing it according to the various rows of orisha goods. I can tell by the way he says each item's correct name that he loves what he does.

"Señor Miguel, how did you start this store?" I ask as he fills the basket. Mama's slightly ahead of us, adding to her already long list.

"That's a good question, Jayd," Miguel says, inspecting his products. He sees a candle for Legba turned the wrong way and immediately aligns it with the rest of the row before answering my question. "When *mi familia* first opened this botanica, it was much smaller. We rented a storefront around the corner from our home in Lynwood. When it opened, we had a huge fiesta and invited all the neighbors to come and visit the store. We had plenty of food and gave away candles and incense. The drummers and dancers kept the party going all night. I mean, we had a really good time."

"We sure did," Mama says, continuing her shopping while strolling down memory lane with Miguel. I didn't even think she was listening, the way she's carefully inspecting each item before passing it to Miguel. She bends down to pick up a case of white candles, but Miguel spots it and insists on getting it for her.

"Unfortunately, the only thing the neighbors remembered about that store was the fact that we had live chickens in a cage in the back. For years to come, they would whisper about what we did when we held ceremonies, even though none of them ever stepped foot in our store again."

"They made your lives a living hell, but we fixed them," Mama says, smiling knowingly at Miguel, who shares the same spark in his brown eyes. I'm curious to know the details, but

I know better than to interrupt when Mama's speaking. She picks up several boxes of coconut incense, a favorite of both Obatala and the ancestors. It's also good for general shrine use.

"Yes, we did. But we suffered through years of police raids because of the vicious accusations by our neighbors. They said we were eating chicken hearts whole and sacrificing our young. It was awful." We turn the corner, almost running into a lady and her basket. There are several customers shopping and in line for the cashier. Like at Netta's salon, Saturday's a profitable day for this store.

"Ignorance is harmful, Jayd. Remember that." Mama's got that right. The past week in school has proven that point well.

"When clients would come into the store sometimes they would be harassed and called devil worshippers by people on the street. One client told me that one of the oldest and bitterest of all the neighbors would feign ignorance that the store existed when asked for directions. One time she even had the nerve to ask the client why he wanted that kind of store. Didn't he know they sold live chickens in there? The client responded by saying he likes his meat fresh and the old lady went on with her gardening, without saying another word," Miguel says, getting a good laugh at the thought.

"Yes, thank God some of our devotees are strong in their faith," Mama says, checking her list one last time before heading to one of the three cashiers at the counter behind the bulletproof glass.

"Yes, little Jayd, when Legba opened the road for us to get a bigger, more centrally located space, we decided to name it for our collective walk as orisha worshippers and keep botanica out of the name. We can't argue with ignorance, nor do we want any of our clients harassed while shopping for supplies," Miguel says, securing Mama's place in line. He would

take her to the back and ring her up ahead of the other customers, but Mama refuses to accept special treatment.

"And we're glad, too," Mama says, pushing the basket up
to be third in line. "Because of your dedication we have one
of the best botanicas in Los Angeles County—run by a true
devotee, not a mercenary like most of the other shops I visit."
Watching Mama and Miguel continue their chatter, my thoughts
drift off to what the people outside are saying about The
Path. There's a church across the street that looks like it's just
ending or beginning Saturday night service. Some of the
church folks are outside staring and pointing across the street.
I'm sure Miguel and his regulars are used to the gawking by
now, but I'm not. It makes me uncomfortable having vehe-
ment hate directed my way, no matter where it's coming from.

Most of the patrons of any botanica are Hispanic, with
black clientele taking a distant second place. And the people
in most neighborhoods in LA County realize the tension between the two cultures. I don't understand why so many
black people hate Mexicans. If it weren't for stores like this
one, there would be very little representation of our tradi-
tions around. By having botanicas and practitioners of the
faith in our neighborhood, they bring a little bit of Africa to
the hood, and I'm grateful for it, no matter what country
they're from or what language they speak.

Mama finally makes it to the front of the line and pays for
all of the supplies. Miguel walks us to the car and helps us
load the trunk and backseat before saying good-bye to Mama
and hello to the haters across the street. As they hiss at us,
Mama looks at them and smiles, all the while holding on to
the multiple eleke—each beaded necklace representing a
particular Orisha—hanging around her neck.

"Mama, how can you be so calm when people are so rude?"
I ask, driving out of the crowded lot as quickly as I can. It's
time to get out of this part of the city and back to Compton.

After I drop Mama off I'm going straight to my mom's and curling up on the couch with the remote and a bag of Trader Joe's Joe-Joe's—double-chocolate flavor. I found my mom's secret stash last weekend and have been waiting for the perfect time to dig in.

"Oshune is mostly about love and forgiveness, Jayd. Being sweet is the best way to ensure victory in any situation. And I've told you many times, Jayd. Be audacious in your faith. Speak for your ancestors and they will take care of you. They—like the Orisha—need us to be their vessels. If we don't honor them, they'll be lost forever. That's why I don't initiate non-Africans into the religion. I believe everyone should honor their respective ancestors, period. And I like to think that by turning away folks, I'm helping them to discover their true path."

"But if they're called to the religion, does it matter that they're white?" I ask, playing devil's advocate and thinking of Chance and his true roots. "Maybe they have a little black in them we can't see."

Mama carefully contemplates before answering my question. I turn onto Alondra Boulevard and head straight for Gunlock Avenue. It's pretty much a straight shot from the botanica to Mama's house.

"You remember that book I used to read to you when you were a little girl, about the little chicken who went around looking for his mother? But the whole time his mother was preparing his dinner, and had the chicken been patient and waited she would've come right back?"

"Yeah, I remember that one," I say, reminiscing about our story time. Mama reading to me was my favorite part of our nightly routine when I was a child. "I loved that book."

"I know you did because it was relevant then, like it is now. White folks can look through as many doors as they want to, even voodoo and other traditional African religions. But no

matter what they think, voodoo is not their mother." Mama
has a special way of making sense so that even a baby can understand. Noticing the novel Ms. Toni gave me on the floor
next to her feet, she picks it up and reads the description on
the back cover. She then tosses the borrowed text in the
backseat, hissing her teeth. That can't be a good sign. I was
hoping she'd love the book like I do and want to read it together, maybe even form our own book club based on the
women in our lineage. But I guess that won't be happening
anytime soon.

"We also have to be careful about stereotyping ourselves
within the caricatures of the religion given to us by people
who misinterpret voodoo. We're not mammies and this ain't
no magic show. And more often than not, any movie or novel
that mentions voodoo does so from a horror, blood-and-guts
perspective. And that's not how we roll." Mama always makes
me laugh when she talks in slang like me and my friends.

"I hear you, Mama, loud and clear." We pull up to the dark
house and notice no one's home. Everyone else must be out
for the night already. I back the car into the driveway, ready
to unload the trunk and get on with our evening. It's dark
and the nightly chill is unwelcoming without a jacket to keep
me warm.

I'm surprised Mama didn't complain about my driving. I'll
take her silence as a compliment.

"Do you know how many times I read about misrepresen-
tations of our lineage in some book and get vexed?" Mama
asks, glancing at the book in the back before exiting the passenger's side. "Maman Marie was not a witch, and that's what
most of these people out here think. It gets on my nerves
and it hurts. But it also keeps me on my toes. If we don't live
her truth and the truth of other devotees, then who will?"

I unload the objects from the trunk and follow Mama to
the spirit room. I get her message loud and clear. I have to

find another way to deal with Reid and his bull besides crippling him in public. I'll take the rest of the weekend to think about how to do that and how to be successful with the ASU. Right now, I just want to finish my work and head to my mom's. Monday will come soon enough.

~ 5 ~
Bunny Boilers

*"Don't know how you do the voodoo that you do/
But hell, this is swell."*

—SALT-N-PEPA

I successfully avoided talking to Rah for the entire week-end—a major feat. In order for me to get my work done, I had to take some time alone. That meant no girls or boys to distract me from my goals. And because I was so disciplined with my one day off from the outside world, I was able to work on my English paper, get some studying done for the rest of my classes, as well as record this past week's experiences in my spirit journal. After all of my major tasks were out of the way, I snuck in some reading time for *Voodoo Dreams* before calling it a night.

When I arrived on campus this morning and saw that ASB was already busy posting the flyers for Cultural Awareness Day, I felt a renewed sense of responsibility to our new club. I want to make sure the African Student Union starts out with a bang at the festival. I also want to make Mr. A and Ms. Toni are proud of me. Mama's slightly disappointed in my choice of pleasure reading, but I'm actually learning a lot from this novel. Maybe Mr. Adewale and Ms. Toni would like to start a book club separate from what we're doing in ASU, since Mama's not feeling me. There are lessons to be gained from Ms. Toni's bookshelf, whether or not she likes the packaging.

The first two class periods were quite busy. And I spent

the nutrition break doing research in the library, where I also ate a Snickers without anyone noticing. My sugar rush is in full effect, and I'm anxious to utilize my energy in debate class. Mr. Adewale's got this morning's topic on the board. Based on the words written in blue marker on the white board, I know today's debate will be anything but friendly. I can already feel all eyes on me, and I'm ready for any hater who comes my way.

"So should we all be one or two religions, like political parties?" Mr. Adewale asks, setting the debate off. I look around the quiet room waiting for someone to take the lead. No one's speaking so I guess I'll have to.

"No, because my religion would go back into hiding like it was forced to do when my ancestors were captives in this country." I shudder at the thought of not being able to practice voodoo as we now know it. Mama had to hide it under the cloak of Catholicism when she was a child, and then again when she got older, under the guise of being a first lady of the AME church. But now we're free to just be ourselves and damned proud of it, too.

"Aren't you Christian like the rest of us?" Alia asks, assuming something I never told her. Most people think that all black people belong to a Christian church, whatever the denomination. But not this black girl.

"No, I am not a Christian. Never have been and never will be." All eyes are now on me, the heathen in the room. The only proud eyes I see staring back at me are Mr. Adewale's, Maggie's, and Emilio's. Jeremy looks bored with the conversation and puts his head down on his desk, ready for a quick nap. Since he's a self-proclaimed atheist, I'm sure Jeremy finds this debate futile.

"Then what religion are you?" Alia's question hits me like a ton of bricks. Should I out myself right here, right now?

There's really no use in avoiding it any longer. Everyone up here knows I walk differently, and they all have their suspicions about me being a witch. But to actually claim my voodoo crown is another thing entirely.

I look around at the thirty-plus faces staring at me, waiting for my reply. Will they understand the difference between a priestess and a witch, or brush it off like Jeremy did when I told him why I didn't want to see the stupid Valentine's Day movie he suggested? Even after Mama and Netta's pep talk on Saturday, I still don't know how to respond. Mama would wring my neck if she could see me now.

"I don't think so, lil miss," my mom says. *"She'd be proud of you for owning your crown, as long as you keep your mouth shut about the ins and outs of how our house works. But she'd never object to you claiming your heritage."* Without reservation, Mama said to be bold in my faith. Here goes nothing.

"Thank you, Mom. I needed that," I quickly think back, now ready to answer the question.

"I practice traditional West African spirituality, also known as voodoo in the Americas and across the rest of the African diaspora."

"Oh," Alia says, backing up from me a little bit. Everyone seems to have taken a deep breath at my confession. I feel like I'm on the witness stand and my classmates are the jury.

"Across the what?" Del asks. He's not the only one who looks confused.

"The African diaspora," I repeat, much to Mr. Adewale's liking. He's sitting back in his seat, enjoying the debate. "It's the trail of blood that followed the slave ships from Africa." The shocked expressions on most of the students' faces tells me I've struck a chord.

"Excuse me, Mr. Adewale," a student from the main office

says from outside of the open classroom door. "I need you to sign something." The timid girl walks in and hands our teacher the paper.

"I'll be right back, class. Please continue the discussion." Mr. Adewale looks at the letter and follows the girl out of the room. Whatever it says must be pretty private for him to leave his post at such a volatile point in the conversation.

"Don't y'all kill chickens and drink their blood?" Laura asks, now officially offending me. Apparently Emilio's feeling me, too. Jeremy hasn't stopped staring at me since my open admission of being a priestess shocked him awake. Although I hate being in the center of a negative spotlight, I'm glad the truth is finally out. Misty looks uncomfortable with the direction of the conversation and mentally checks out by reading the textbook. Misty can continue to live in fear if she wants to. Like Mama said, we don't need to hide behind white gods anymore, and I'm ready to remove my veil, dead chickens and all.

"No, we only do that to stupid white girls who ask dumbass questions," I say, the anger apparent in my voice. Emilio smiles at me and knows that I just want to put the fear of God in this girl. She already knows how I get down, from firsthand experience.

"Jayd, you really need to speak with someone about your anger issues," Reid cautiously adds. From the dull look in his blue eyes, I can tell he's still shook up from the mental ass-whipping I gave him last week. But little does he know I already have had counseling and it did no good. These people up here can still get a rise out of me because their ignorance of other cultures is so shocking. If it doesn't look, walk, and talk like they do, they have no respect for it.

"You know, in my village we raise our own food, vegetables, and livestock. It's just a part of our daily lives. And it's also a part of our religion. It seems that here in the United

States most people are disconnected from their roots, and that is sad," Emilio says, offering me his support from across the classroom, making Jeremy jealous.

"Yes, and your people also boil rabbits and frogs and dogs and shit in your little third world country," Laura says, eliciting laughter from her wicked crew. "But that's not how we do it in the first world." Emilio looks like he wants to slap the spit out of Laura's mouth, but luckily Mr. Adewale walks back into the classroom just in time to cool our heated discussion.

"Okay, so what did I miss?" Mr. A asks, obviously disturbed by whatever news he received from the main office. However, he's excited that we're debating without him. I don't know why. Nothing productive is coming from this conversation at all.

"You missed this girl calling my people bunny boilers and Jayd a chicken-blood drinker or something like that." With Emilio's thick Spanish accent, even the most offensive words now possess a sexy tone. "Where do you all get your information about traditional religions from? Is this the type of education I left Venezuela for?" Emilio's right. The only thing he can learn at this school is how to be a racist, seriously.

"Okay, let's all calm down and take it from the top. The original topic of debate for the week, is how does learning about other cultures influence your worldview? And if the influence is positive or negative. Today's specific topic is, should we have two official religions, or more, in the United States?" Mr. Adewale says, pointing to the newspaper article he's holding up. "This is real, people."

"Like I said, I think other cultures can learn a great deal from us about how to behave in a modern society," Laura says, sticking her narrow nose up in the air higher than the stick already up her ass. "And we can learn from others just how lucky and advanced we are." Laura's a bitch and then some.

"Others should be so lucky that they can come here and mesh with us. We're so giving," Cameron says—the newest member of the bitch crew. Laura's clone sounds just as clueless as the prototype.

"Yeah, and everyone knows how primitive third world countries are. And the fact that we saved all of those other less fortunate people you'd think would earn us some respect. But all we ever hear in return is complaint after compliant." Reid is really smelling himself today. Since my extra sight has been suppressed, maybe I should find another way to remind him of his recent lesson in humility. Seems he didn't learn anything the first time around.

"What is this idea of 'others' floating around this room?" Mr. Adewale asks, visually upset with that word. "Before I stepped outside, you were talking about all Americans melting into one citizen of the Untied States, Reid. What happened?" KJ and his crew are obviously tired—from a weekend of hardcore partying, I assume. It's March Madness time and his basketball buddies at UCLA probably allowed him to hang with the big boys. Mr. A looks around the class but no one is saying a word.

"I do believe that. But some people don't want to give up their primitive ways to assimilate," Reid says, looking directly at me. There's that word again. Too bad I can't use Maman's powers, because if I could, he'd be squirming on the floor like a python by now.

"There you go with that Borg talk. Give *Star Trek* a rest, please," I say, taking Ms. Toni's novel out and placing it on the desk in front of me so I don't forget to return it at lunch. "Pick up a book for a change. I have an entire list of authors who would counter your thought process. They've dealt with your kind before." I'm so sick of this debate I would walk out if it were any other teacher. But I know Mr. A must be going somewhere with this, so I'll stick it out.

"My kind?" Reid repeats. "You see that, right there. If I'd said something like that I'd immediately be called a racist. But because I'm a white man and you're a black woman, you'll never wear that title."

"Damn skippy," Nigel says, having my back while rubbing Mickey's belly. She couldn't care less about the conversation, but I'm glad someone does because the rest of the black folks up in this class are too quiet for me today. I know it's Monday, but damn. These folk around here need to wake up in more ways than one.

"I'm not talking about your kind from a racial point of view," I say, pointing at Reid, who is sitting directly across from me. "I'm talking about your ignorant kind. And trust, ignorance crosses racial lines," I say, eyeing KJ, Misty, and the rest of their silent crew. They look at me, knowing I've just busted them out. They know as little about African American history as any of the white students up in here. That much is evident from our first ASU meeting last week.

"I hear that," Emilio says. I'm glad he's talkative about what he knows. It's refreshing to hear his point of view and always lovely to watch him do his confident thang. Jeremy watches me watching our classmate, the jealousy rising in his now wide-awake eyes. What can I say? I like an intelligent man, and Jeremy's not the only one walking around this campus who can hold his own on a variety of topics. I bet Emilio can even play chess as well as Jeremy, if not better. That would really piss Jeremy off.

"You hear what? The sounds of dogs screaming when they see you coming?" Reid says, making his crew laugh. Before Mr. Adewale can defend him, Emilio catches the insult rebound and serves it back up court.

"Not any louder than my people scream when they see your people coming," Emilio says, his bright eyes beaming. He's so on point with his game this morning. "The massacre isn't over, you know. Only in this country can a man who got lost, misnamed the countries that he visited, exterminated their populations, and then claimed them as gifts for his queen get a national holiday named for him. No wonder little Bush was your president for two terms." Those historical facts shut Reid and his howling hyenas up, for the time being. Mr. Adewale looks proud of his new protégé and I'm proud of him, too.

"Whatever. All I know is that my neighbor had an affair with her gardener a couple of years back, and in a jealous rage he almost choked her to death," Laura says. "After that incident, my father promised never to hire an immigrant to work at our home ever again."

"What the hell is your point?" I ask Laura, unsure how her both classist and racist comment relates to the topic at hand. Mr. Adewale shakes his head in frustration. I know he wants to cuss her out for that one, but can't because he needs his job.

"My point is that everyone knows how jealous Latinos can be."

"Have you ever seen *Fatal Attraction*?" I ask the stupid broad. "That was all about white folks and I think it was the chick who was boiling bunny rabbits, not the gardener," I say, making the nonwhite majority in class laugh. At least they're all awake.

"Whatever, Jayd. That was a movie. I'm talking about reality."

"And the reality is that you just classified an isolated incident and made a case for an entire culture to be deemed as irrational beings. If that's how we're rationalizing issues, then let's start with why black women have been raped for centuries by white men. Does that mean that all white men are rapists?" Reid, Jeremy, and Nigel look at me like I just dropped a bomb in the middle of the room, each staring at me for their own reasons. Nigel smiles at me, shaking his head in agreement.

"Okay, that's the bell. We'll continue this discussion tomorrow. Come prepared to prove your points of view through resources other than your personal opinions," Mr. Adewale says, acknowledging the loud ring filling the tense air. Reid's bright red face gives his humiliation away. He was one-upped by the new boy and the black girl and there's nothing he can do about it. "And please remember to stay focused on the topic, even though it's okay to deviate slightly. Good class," he says as the students file out of the room. I'm ready to enjoy a quiet lunch. All of this arguing has worked up quite an appetite.

Jeremy nods good-bye to me as he heads out of the room ahead of me. I guess we won't be spending lunch together. He probably needs some time to process what he just heard. Mickey and Nigel are spending lunch together off campus, and so are Nellie and Chance. It's apparently couples day and I've been left out of the group. But that's okay. I'm sure I'll find something to get into if I set my mind to it. A girl like me is never single for long unless it's by choice. And right now, I choose to honor my hunger and worry about the rest later.

Monday was such an intense day that the rest of the week has been mild, comparatively speaking. After dealing with meetings and work all week, I'm looking forward to the last two days of the week going by just as quickly. And so far, today has also been a chill day, especially since our regularly scheduled AP lunch meeting was cancelled.

Yesterday's ASU meeting was much less eventful than the first because about a third less students showed up. I knew that would happen. Shae, Tony, and a few others from South Central decided more reading wasn't important on their to-do list, but KJ and his boys stuck it out, with Misty dutifully right behind him. Emilio, Chance, and Alia also showed up to our second meeting, which was a good thing. We need the multicultural balance in the room.

With me, Nigel, and Mickey also in attendance, Nellie was the only one missing from our crew. She's been acting a little reserved ever since Mickey and I checked her for calling us bitches, not that it's stopped Nellie from being her regular bougie self. Jeremy has also kept his distance, only speaking to me to say "hi" and "bye" when I do see him third and fourth period. I don't know if he's mostly upset about my being a voodoo priestess or because Emilio's obviously got the hots for me. I'm sure it's a little of both. Jeremy really needs to grow the hell up and get over it.

I make my way through the lunch crowd and into the main hall to switch out my books for tonight's homework and to again attempt returning Ms. Toni's book. As usual, she's been hard to catch all week.

"Hi, Jayd," Emilio says, approaching me as I continue sifting through the various notebooks and papers littering my locker. Someone should really organize this thing.

"Hey, Emilio. What's up?" I ask, closing my locker door and readjusting the heavy backpack on my shoulders. I already have my lunch so all I need to do now is find a spot to chill for the next half hour.

"Would you mind if I joined you for lunch?" the cute sophomore asks. I look around the emptying hall, trying to buy time to make up an excuse because I do want to be alone. But on second thought, I can see no reason why I shouldn't have lunch with Emilio.

"Not at all," I say, allowing him to take my backpack and lead the way outside. It's a nice day to relax in the sun.

Emilio finds a shady spot under a tree not far from the entrance to the main hall. I don't usually like to sit where there's a lot of foot traffic, but this spot will do. He takes out his lunch, which consists of a sandwich and chips he just bought from the cafeteria. His food looks much more filling than my chosen banana and Doritos with the bottled water I bought during snack time. Maybe he'll give me a bite of his sub if I ask real nice.

"So how are you enjoying our crazy campus?" I ask between bites. He unwraps his sandwich and starts eating it like he's as hungry as I am. On second thought, maybe I won't beg for his lunch. At the rate he's grubbing, it looks like he's going to be finished before I am.

"It's a beautiful school, esthetically speaking," he says, looking at all of the white students enjoying the day. We won't see any students with skin tones close to ours unless we venture over to the main lunch quad near the cafeteria, where South Central and El Barrio—the Latino clique—congregate on a regular basis. "But the culture is a bit strange for me. And everyone keeps treating me like I don't know anything. I guess it's the accent," he says, smiling at me. I know how Emilio feels. My first week at South Bay High was a culture shock, too, and I'm still feeling it a year and a half later.

"Trust, the school has earned the nickname Drama High." Emilio looks at me curiously. Do I have something in my teeth?

"What is this 'Drama High' name for?" Emilio's innocence is so cute, but I'll keep that to myself, just in case he takes the intended compliment as demeaning. I don't want him to feel like I'm treating him the way some of the ignorant students do.

"It's just a title the school has earned since its inception, I'm guessing. But I never questioned it because it's true."

"Yeah. There's something very different about the way these white Americans with money act. My last student exchange program took me to Puerto Rico. It was like a home away from home." Emilio finishes the last bite of his food and moves on to his Dr Pepper.

"So do you consider yourself black?" I had to ask, especially after that comment he made about white folks. Emilio looks like a fine young black man with hella curly hair to me. But I want to be sure he sees the same thing.

"Do I have a choice?" he asks, tickled by my question. "In this political environment, anyone with African blood is black, and I am definitely of African descent."

"I figured as much," I say. I'm glad Emilio stood up for his people in class the other day. I'm also glad he identifies with being black, which I wasn't really sure of before. Some South Americans call themselves black and others don't. Being black is about more than skin color and hair texture: it's also about claiming an identity rooted in the recognition of a shared survival.

"I liked what you had to say about the religion in class on Monday," he says, lowering his voice as any practitioner with the proper training would when talking about orisha worship.

"Are you familiar with the orisha?" I ask, curious if he's been a quiet priest all these weeks. It would be cool to have another ally on campus other than our teacher, Mr. Adewale.

"Yes, I practice Santeria, the way of the saints," Emilio says, pulling his shirt collar down, revealing a brown and green eleke. "I'm a child of Ifa."

"Ashe," I say, smiling at our secret. I knew there was something special about Emilio. His eyes are piercing and his energy calm. Yes, Emilio is definitely a child of Ifa or Orunmilla, the prophet of the religion, who is known for his controlled behavior.

"I was so impressed that you—an American descendant of slavery—knew about our ancestors' ways. Most of you do not," Emilio says, no longer sounding as cute as he did a few minutes ago. His head may be cool, but it's big.

"Excuse me?" I ask, ready to show him how we get down on this side of the world. But he continues with his conceited view like I didn't say a word.

"*Mi abuelita* always says African Americans really know nothing about the religion. She also says that we—the Africans in the South Americas and Cuba—saved the orisha. If it were left up to the Africans here, there would be no more santos." I want to slap Emilio so bad right now I can feel the hot flesh on my cheeks fully exposed.

"Do you believe everything your grandmother tells you?" I ask.

"Of course I do. Don't you?" he asks, as serious as a heart attack.

"Hell no," I say. I didn't mean it like that, but I do have a mind of my own. If I'd shared Mama's opinion about reading novels about our lineage, I would've never read the book Ms. Toni let me borrow. And that would have been my bad.

"Well, my grandmother never lies to me about anything," Emilio says, dusting grass off his jeans and bringing his knees up to his chest. "And she knows everything there is to know about the religion." His blind allegiance is slightly dramatic and scary.

"What the hell are you talking about? Just because American blacks don't express it the same way y'all do doesn't mean that we don't honor our ancestors. Look at our history. We've always been root workers, obeah women and priestesses. We call it voodoo and speak Creole, Ebonics and whatever other language we could use to survive," I say, giving him a quick lesson in African American culture. He needs to check his ego at the curb when talking about us like he's an expert.

"Whatever you say, Jayd, and I don't want to argue with you," Emilio says, putting up his hands in mock surrender like we do in debate class when one person gives in to the other's reasoning. But I know that's not what's going on here. "The difference between my culture and yours is that we never left our gods. And in return they never left us. Can blacks in this country say the same thing? I think not." Emilio's a cocky little something when it comes to his South American orisha culture, I see. And he's also a grandmama's boy in a very dependent way that is very unattractive. I'm glad we had this little chat. I see that even though we're both from essentially the same culture, we're still on different sides.

The bell rings, leaving me to think about what Emilio just said. Part of me actually agrees with him and that pisses me off. I'm a grandmama's girl, but not to the point where I think that Mama shits gold. The after-lunch rush to fifth period has begun and we'd better join the flow of bodies if we're going to make it to class on time.

"Until next time, sweet Jayd," Emilio says, taking both of my hands in his and pulling me into a kiss. I give in to his soft, sweet lips momentarily before punching him in the chest and pulling away from his embrace.

"What the hell was that?" I shout, making my way up from the grassy spot. Jeremy hears my loud voice and starts walking across the quad to where we're standing. Good. Maybe he can save the tail end of this lunch break by finally apologizing for his strange behavior this week.

"I've been waiting to do that all my life," Emilio says, looking pleased with his rude behavior. "Have you ever seen *The Cosby Show*? Ever since seeing that television show I've liked black American girls. And you are so beautiful," he says, coming in for round two—but it ain't happening.

"Emilio, you can't just go around kissing on people without their permission," I say, picking up my belongings and punching him one more time. Jeremy arrives just as I land the blow.

"Oh, Jayd, you hurt me so sweet," Emilio says, feigning hurt while holding my fist to his chest. This fool is crazy.

"So now you're hanging out with him?" Jeremy asks. I thought he was coming over here to rescue me, not yell at me. Oh no, not another confrontation. I look at both Jeremy and Emilio and realize that I'm wasting my time and energy fighting with these clueless dudes.

"Who I hang with is my business, Jeremy," I say, passing them both by and heading for class with the rest of the student population. They can argue with each other. It seems like Jeremy and I never talk anymore, just go back and forth about one thing or another. What happened to my friend I could have interesting debates and good chess matches with?

I attempt to continue my trek in solitude, but Jeremy's not having it. He follows me down the hill toward the drama room and away from Emilio and his *novela* now costarring me. The drama never seems to end.

"Jayd, we're having a conversation. You can't just walk away from me," Jeremy says, grabbing me by the arm. Oh no he didn't go there with me.

"Look, Chris Brown, you need to let go before you find yourself laid out on the cement," I say, snatching my arm away from him. Jeremy looks truly shocked by his own action. I guess he's never had a girl walk away from him before. All I can say is *welcome to dating a black girl* because we usually don't stay around and get yelled at unless we're yelling back.

"Jayd, I saw you kissing Emilio," Jeremy says, his tone deeper than I've ever heard him speak to me before. "Are you seriously telling me that you and he are hanging out now?" What's gotten into him? He's been aloof lately, even for him. But this rage is coming out of nowhere, especially since he's well aware that I'm kicking it with Rah, too.

"What if we are, Jeremy? Are you going to snatch him up, too? Because I've already been in a relationship like that and I'm not going back there again." As a matter of fact, most of the dudes I hang with are a bit on the jealous side. And by a bit I mean they don't want anyone else touching their girls.

"You know what you are, Jayd? A tease," Jeremy says with all of the venom of a scorpion dripping from his words. Me, a tease? All I did was accept a lunch invitation. How did we get here? "From now on you can kiss whomever you like. I'm done being your bitch," he says, storming off toward the parking lot. I guess he's not going to class this afternoon. I've never seen him so mad at me before. And I've never heard him refer to himself as anyone's bitch. What the hell just happened?

I should know how to control my temper because of what it can do to my ashe, just like I should know better by now than to trust Rah with my heart. Luckily I don't have to work at Netta's this evening, leaving me free to go home early and relax. Maybe I'll even bake something sweet for myself that'll help shake this negative school day off of me.

It's a bright sunny day and I'm glad for it. I love to sit out in the sun on days like this, pop in my headphones and let the music on my iPod carry me off to a place where I can just be, especially when I get home early enough to enjoy the last hour of sunlight. It never lasts for too long, but it's nice to steal a moment to myself every now and then. I have some school and spirit work to catch up on and could use the peace to get it done.

"Don't sit out here too long," my cousin Jay says, passing me by on his way up the front porch heading toward the front door. I guess he decided to hang out late after school. "You're already black enough."

"What the hell is that supposed to mean?" I wish these headphones could block out ignorance, but they're not magic. I try to focus on my English paper rough draft, but it's no use with Jay around.

"You know what I mean. You're out here getting a tan. I know you go to school with white folks, but don't forget you ain't one of them." Jay smacks me on the head and I return the love by tripping him on his way across the threshold into the house. He looks back and smiles at me, indicating his surrender, just like I thought he would. We used to fight hardcore when we were kids, and I was always the victor. Not because he was weak, but more because I'm relentless when it comes to winning, no matter the game.

"Jay, the sun is good for us. And you could use a little sun yourself, with your pale, ashy elbows sticking out for all to see," I say to his back as he closes the security screen, which is the only thing separating us.

"Better to be ashy than dark," Jay says, repeating thousands of years of self-hatred. Jay takes a seat at the dining room table on the other side of the screen and sifts through the mail like we all do. There's very little privacy in this house.

"So you're saying my mom and your grandfather would be better off ashy?" I don't know why I'm even entertaining this fool this afternoon. But Mr. Adewale says we have to take the opportunity to educate whenever possible and my big cousin definitely needs it. I can't believe he's a senior in high school. He acts more immature than a sophomore. Speaking of which, my phone vibrates on my leg and Emilio's name pops up on the screen. After today's surprise kiss, I haven't answered a single one of his ten calls.

"They were born that way," he says matter-of-factly. "They can't help being on the darker side. But you're just tempting fate. What, are you trying to get darker so you can feel more black, Harriet Tubman?" I can't believe how stupid my cousin can be at times.

"I'm surprised you know who she is." Sometimes attending a black high school does have its perks, even if Compton High School's mascot is a Tarbabe. I don't know what to make of it, but Mama said that for years she and Daddy led a protest to change that when they first moved here. They eventually gave up, since they were the only ones who really cared about the racist implication of the word.

"There's a lot I know. You should take notes," Jay says, leaving the dining room to go shit, shower, and shave—his usual evening routine. Even with eight people living here, we all try to honor each other's bathroom time. Why my grandparents never built a second bathroom onto the house is beyond me. But when things get really bad, me and Mama use the half-bath in the backhouse. There's no shower, but it takes care of everything else. When the sun sets, I'll head to the spirit room and finish my work back there. The faster I get done the quicker I can go to sleep.

Even with all of the work I had to do this week I reread portions of the novel I borrowed from Ms. Toni since she was missing in action. It's Friday and I don't want to go another weekend holding on to her book or I'm liable to never give it back. I don't like keeping other people's things for too long, but every time I went to her office she was out. I'm sure she's extra busy, with the festival right around the corner. And now that she's one of the advisers for the African Student Union, I'm sure she's busy trying to get the club legitimized so that we can participate in the festivities, too.

Once I started reading *Voodoo Dreams* I couldn't put it down. I've never read a book like that before. It's strange reading a fictitious account of my lineage, especially the sections where the characters were dreaming and one ancestor took over the other's body. But it's always interesting to see how other people see the religion and the priestesses within it. Unlike this author's account, Mama sticks to the African side of our heritage, completely eliminating the use of European saints in place of our orishas. And I'm glad for it because I—like Mama—don't see the need for masking our true selves.

"Hey, Ms. Toni," I say, knocking on her office door before entering the cozy space. The soothing sound of Miles Davis floats through the computer speakers on her desk, welcoming me into her space. I'm glad I finally caught her.

"Miss Jackson. It's nice to see you this morning," she says, standing up behind her desk and reaching over to hug me. As I embrace her thin, tall frame, I swear Ms. Toni's lost weight since I last saw her, which was only a week ago. If I didn't know any better I'd say she got a hold of that pipe. But I know she's too smart for that kind of bull.

"How are you feeling, Ms. Toni? Are these people up here working you too hard?" I look into her sad brown eyes and can tell she's losing sleep at night, just like Mama does when she's overworked. Between caring for her two young daughters and mourning her slain husband who was killed in an accident years ago, I know Ms. Toni doesn't get much rest. I wish there was something I could do to help her. For now I will keep her in my prayers.

"Oh, girl, I'm just fine. How are you?" She sits back down at her desk and wraps the cashmere shawl around her body. The cream colored fabric looks radiant against her chocolate skin.

"I'm good," I say, taking the thick novel out of my backpack and passing it to her. "Thank you for the great read. It was definitely captivating." Ms. Toni takes the book from me and smiles.

"I thought you might like it." What else did Mr. A tell her about me? "Anytime you want to borrow a book you know you're more than welcome."

"I'll have to take you up on that more often. I've been slipping on my pleasure reading this year." I miss checking books out from her personal library. But she never shared these types of texts with me before. I'm curious to know what Mr. Adewale has shared with her about my lineage. The next time I have a minute alone with Mr. A, he's getting grilled.

"Well, I have a feeling this was more than a pleasure read for you, Miss Jayd." I look at her smiling back at me, and know she knows more than I've ever shared with her.

"Yes, it was." Unsure of what to say next, I quietly eye the books on the tall shelf next to her desk. I see many titles of interest, but will wait until another time for my next borrowed item.

"You know, I don't know everything about what you and Mr. Adewale share, but I know enough to believe you when you say there's nothing inappropriate going on," Ms. Toni says, breaking the silence.

"And I hope you know me well enough to know I would never betray your trust," I say.

"Trust is mutual, Jayd. Next time give me a little more faith, okay?" The bell rings for third period and our conversation is unfortunately cut short. Lord knows I'd rather stay in here with Ms. Toni than go to government class with Mrs. Peterson, any day.

"Okay, Ms. Toni. And that goes for you, too. If you have any questions from now on I'll answer them to the best of my ability." I can't tell her everything, but I'll do my best to disclose any pertinent information without lying. I give her a hug and head out of the ASB room and into the main hall. Nellie and Mickey are waiting at my locker. I hope they weren't waiting there for long.

"What's up with y'all?" I ask, approaching my girls. I only have a minute or two to catch up. Chance and I are rehearsing at lunch and can't afford any interruptions, which also means nosy significant others can't watch us. I hope Nellie's not pissed about it and here to tell me off in her own bougie way.

"What's up is my baby shower," Mickey says. Is she serious? We all have to be in class now, and she's worried about a party? This girl really needs to get her priorities straight.

"Yes, and it's going to be fabulous," Nellie says with stars in her eyes. Party planning is her thing. I guess that's why she's so attracted to ASB. That and the fact she gets to hang out with the rich kids.

"I'm not talking about this now. I have to get to class," I say, speeding up ahead of them.

"Can you meet up this weekend and talk about the shower? We really need to get started on the guest list," Nellie yells after me. Mickey's too busy wolfing down her box of Lemonheads to speak up.

"I don't know. I have to work all weekend, both at the shop and at home. But I'll see if I can," I yell back.

"What about tonight? Chance and Nigel are playing ball at the courts by Nigel's house. We can chat while the boys play." I can see Nellie's not letting me out of this one. My girls are persistent when it comes to what they want. And if Mickey wants a shower and Nellie wants to throw it, it will be done. And I, as a loyal friend, will no doubt be dragged into it somehow. All I'm worried about right now is making it through the rest of the day. If I have to agree to give up my free night, so be it.

"Fine, I'll see y'all later." Damn, now can I get to class? On my way down the history hall I feel someone on my tail. Maybe it's Jeremy, also on his way to class. He'd better not come too close to me after the way he treated me yesterday. I don't know what's gotten into him, but he needs to check himself, acting like my daddy and judge all wrapped up in one.

"Hi, Jayd," Emilio says, catching up to me. What the hell does he want now?

"What's happening?" I say without slowing down. The bell should ring any minute and I can't be late. Emilio reaches his hand out to grab mine, but I shy away from his touch.

"I called you. Did you get my messages?" he says, forcing me to stop and deal with him face-to-face. I don't want to be mean, but it seems like that's the only language he'll understand.

"Emilio, I didn't call you back because I was busy," I say. I don't have time to go off on him, nor do I want that kind of attention.

"I know, my sweet. But I still love you," he says, only half joking. Why is this dude feeling me so strongly? I look over Emilio's shoulder to see Jeremy heading this way. I hope he doesn't make another scene like he did on Wednesday.

"Emilio, my love life is complicated and I can't deal with anything new right now. You understand, don't you?" His gorgeous smile quickly morphs into a scowl. Jeremy's almost here and the bell's ringing above our heads, indicating it's time to end this conversation. I glance inside the classroom and notice Mrs. Peterson's not at her desk. The other students wander in and out of the room, taking advantage of the teacher's tardiness. Luckily I won't be marked tardy, but I'd rather be sitting at my desk than outside dealing with this crap.

"I should've known better than to fall for another Oshune girl," Emilio says in a low voice. Who the hell is he getting mad at? After he kissed me without my permission and talked shit about my culture, I should be the one pissed off, not him.

"Hey, I didn't kiss you. You kissed me, and I didn't want it to happen."

"You're crazy, you know that?" Emilio says, his voice get-

ting louder the more red he turns. "That Jeremy was right.
You are a tease, just like all Oshune women are. *Mi abuelita*
was right, as usual." Emilio and his damned grandmother.
Does she walk on water or something?

"First of all, Jeremy and I are friends, and if he wants to go
off on me I can accept it. You, on the other hand, don't know
shit about me or the women in my lineage, so you need to
shut the hell up about it," I say, getting loud right along with
him. I know Jeremy heard us both, and by the way he's charg-
ing toward our classroom, one of us is about to catch his
wrath.

"Is there a problem here?" Jeremy asks, looking from me
to Emilio, unsure of whose side to take this time. I'm glad
he's taking a minute to get his facts straight before pointing
his finger.

"No, there's no problem. It's all my fault," Emilio says, finally backing off and going to his own class. Jeremy looks at
Emilio walk away and then back down at me. I see both re-
morse and anger in his eyes.

"Unnecessary drama, Jayd. That's what you attract," he says
before heading into the classroom. Mrs. Peterson also ap-
proaches the room from the opposite end of the hall where
Emilio's walking. However unfair his words are, Jeremy may
have a point. I do seem to attract drama like bees to honey.
But this was definitely not my fault. Maybe my girls will be
able to help me see my way through this mess when we meet
up later tonight.

It's been too long since I've hung out with my crew on a
Friday night and it's a nice evening to walk through Nigel's
hood, even if the boys did drive to the basketball court only a
few blocks away. Netta gave me tonight off and I graciously
accepted the time, even though I am going to miss the money.
Hopefully I'll make it up tomorrow. I'm working a ten-hour

shift at the shop and I have a few clients lined up in the evening, not to mention the customers I have scheduled for Sunday. It's nice to have an hourly gig, but there's nothing like having a tight side hustle, too.

Chance, Nigel, and Rah are waiting for the court to clear before they can start their game when Mickey, Nelly and I arrive. Nigel thinks he's slick, asking Rah to ball after he found out I was tagging along with my girls. I don't have anything to say to Rah and I hope they both know how serious I am. I need to get rid of some of this heat in my head. Chance and Jeremy both say driving helps them to cool off. Maybe I should try it out for myself. My mom's car is not soothing at all. But one of my friend's cars will do the trick, and Chance's happens to be the closest to where we're posted up. Nellie and Mickey make themselves comfortable on one of the courtside benches while I talk to my boy.

"Can I drive your car?" I ask Chance. He continues revving the engine and with each press on the gas my blood accelerates, too. Something about the sound of him gunning the engine gets me excited.

"Sure, why not?" Chance scoots over to the passenger side and lets me get behind the wheel. Nellie and Mickey are heavily engrossed in baby books, ignoring us completely. I reach down to my left and pull the seat lever to bring myself closer to the foot pedals. At first, I'm shy about pressing on the gas like the owner did. But when I touch my sandals ever-so-slightly to the gas pedal, the rush in my veins forces me to press harder. Nigel and Rah look from the court sidelines at me behind the wheel and shake their heads, smiling at the sight. Where's an outside mirror when a sistah needs one?

"Easy, girl," Chance says, patting my hand and smiling at my obvious excitement. Mickey and Nellie look up from their book, also shaking their heads. This is so much better than picking out hundreds of baby items for Mickey's registry. "Let's take it slow at first and work our way up to the big time, okay?" I put my foot on the brake and ease the automatic transmission out of park. We move slowly at first, admiring the smoothness of the Chevy Nova. The people on the streets look at us as we ride by, eyeing the girl behind the wheel. It feels good, driving in style for a change.

"Okay, let me see what you can do." I catch a glimpse of our reflection in one of the store windows as we cruise down Crenshaw Boulevard. I like what I see and so do the people on the streets. Chance flips a switch and I feel the car's force change. It's like the switch gave it an extra boost or something.

"That's Red Bull for the engine, baby," Chance says, smiling at my surprised expression. "Go ahead, she won't bite." I press on the gas, immediately enticed by the jump in the car's force. Damn, what a rush.

"I don't feel like this when I drive my mom's car," I say, flying down the road like cops don't exist on this block. Right now I couldn't care less about the law. This good feeling is worth the ticket.

"That's because this ain't your mama's car." Chance turns up the OutKast CD and we quickly cruise down the block, impressing the onlookers and waking up sleeping babies as we roll. I used to be annoyed by the sounds hot rods make when they fly down the block but now I understand the allure. This car feels alive, and it feels good to be behind the wheel of such a beast.

When we make it back to the basketball court, Nigel and Rah laugh at my small head poking up from behind the wheel.

"Laugh all y'all want too, but you know I look good," I say out the window as I return the car to its spot. My boys nod in agreement but my girls look mad as hell. I'm not sure if it's because I'm not taking this shower shit seriously or because I took all the attention away from them. The one thing a dude likes more than a fast car is a pretty girl driving it.

"Be careful, Jayd. This type of speed can be very addictive," Chance says, pulling on his Newport. Talk about dangerous addictions. "But I know you can handle it," he adds, impressed by my handling of the car. Nellie looks jealous as all get-out. But if she'd learn how to drive, I'm sure she'd fall in love with the classic vehicle, too. Besides, I need to burn off some steam and this is the safest way to do it. With all that happened this week between me and Jeremy and Emilio, driving that car made it all disappear. But from the way Rah's looking at me, I can tell my good feeling is about to end soon.

~ 6 ~
Not the Mama

*"And girl I wanna be the papa/
You can be the mom."*

—SEAN PAUL

After the game we all walk back to Nigel's house. Living in a nice neighborhood like Lafayette Square affords Nigel the ability to walk down the street to his community park without fear of getting shot by rival gang members and other haters. He can't get too complacent though. Even if they've named their little area, his house is still adjacent to the hood.

When we get back to Nigel's house, Mrs. Esop is outside working in her rose garden. She keeps their yard immaculate. Her roses are as beautiful as the ones Mama grows, but Mrs. Esop's garden is about three times the size of Mama's, making the flowers look more spectacular.

"Jayd, since you know Nigel's mom, it's your job to ask her to come to the shower," Mickey says as we stroll. I'm enjoying our quiet evening, but her idea is ruining my good mood. "My mom's handling the games. Maybe she'll want to help out, too." I look at Mickey and laugh at first, thinking she's joking—but she's not. Doesn't Mickey realize that her dreams of being accepted into the Esop clan are futile?

"Have you completely lost your mind?" I ask, following the boys up the long driveway toward the front door. Nellie looks at us and then back at the catalogue she's studying.

You'd think she was the one having the baby, the way she's picking out the baby's clothes and other necessities.

"No, and you owe it to my soon-to-be-born child Nickey, as her godmother, to make sure that her other grandmother shows up." I know that message is more from my goddaughter than her mother, and neither one of them will be ignored.

"*One* of her godmothers," Nellie says without looking up from her studies. I roll my eyes at both of my girls. Mrs. Esop has been more cordial to me these days, but I still get the feeling she's mad at me for introducing her son to Mickey. I don't know why. It's not like I forced them to sleep together, and that's how they got into this mess.

"Hey, Mom," Nigel says, kissing his mom on the cheek before walking up the front-porch steps. Rah bends down and kisses her other cheek. Chance is new to Nigel's inside crew and simply waves at Mrs. Esop, who returns the gesture.

"Hello, Mrs. Esop," Nellie says, the first of us girls to speak. She looks up from her kneeling position in the grass and smiles at us.

"Hello, ladies," she replies. Mickey looks at me, silently urging me to invite Nigel's mom to the shower. I guess there's no time like the present to attempt the impossible for my girl and her unborn daughter. Nellie and Mickey follow the boys into the house while I stay behind and make small talk with Mrs. Esop.

"I like your roses. The yellow ones are especially nice," I say, smelling the fresh flowers. Mrs. Esop clips one of the full buds and hands it to me. I accept the thoughtful gift, stroking the soft petals against my cheek. My father used to clip roses from his garden and remove the thorns for me when I was a little girl. With the flower tucked behind my ear, I would smile all day long, feeling like I was the prettiest girl in the world.

"Next time you'll have to help me prune them," she says, returning to her gardening. I hate to ruin this bonding moment, but I am here for a purpose.

"Mickey wants to invite you to her baby shower," I blurt out. The sooner I get it over with the quicker I can get back to chilling. The sun is setting and I don't want to be out too late because I have to wake up early in the morning for work. Rah and I haven't had a moment to talk and I want to keep it like that. The last time we were all here together was when I found out about his good—but stupid—deed. I don't want to reenact that dreadful day, nor do I want to talk about it tonight.

"Is that so?" she says, continuing her clipping. "That girl is something else, isn't she?" Mrs. Esop inhales deeply and then exhales, never ceasing her task.

"Yes, she is." I can't help but agree with the truth. Mickey knows she's a lot to handle and wouldn't change her ways for the world. That attitude alone deserves some respect.

"My sorority hosts a cotillion every year. I'm sure Nigel has told you the fun he's had participating as an escort," she says, looking into my eyes. Did she just change the subject on a sistah? What the hell does this have to do with Mickey's shower?

"He has," I say, leaving out the fact that Nigel hates going to the annual debutante ball. And from the way he describes spending an evening with a bunch of bougie, rich black folks, I'm glad I've never had the pleasure of participating in one.

"I think you'd make an excellent candidate for the ball this year, Jayd. Have you ever considered becoming a debutante?" Is she serious?

"No, ma'am, I haven't." I look through the front door at my friends in the foyer, drinking water and snacking on chips while they wait for me to head upstairs, where this evening's session will be held. Now that Sandy's at Rah's crib, I have a feeling we won't be chilling there much as a group—mostly because Nigel can't stand her ass. It's also a given that if I have beef with a chick, then my girls automatically have beef with her, too. And Sandy and I have an entire cattle ranch between the two of us.

Mrs. Esop follows my eyes up the front steps and then returns her focus to her project and to me.

"You're more than what you've become, Jayd," Mrs. Esop says. She again looks toward Rah, Mickey, and the rest of our small crew before returning her gaze to me. "Having babies can wait until after your education."

"I fully agree. I'm not planning on having any kids until well after college," I say. I know I want children, but not anytime soon. Parenting is more than a notion, and an expensive responsibility I don't want on my shoulders right now. That's why I've kept my legs closed, unlike the rest of my friends.

"So you are thinking about college? Good. I'm glad to hear that." She stands up straight, brushing the dirt from her pants and removing her gardening gloves. She's a tall, athletic woman shaped a lot like Michelle Obama. And the way she walks around her home like it's the White House, Mrs. Esop acts like the first lady, too. "I'll make you a deal, Jayd." Uh-oh. I don't like the sound of this.

"Okay," I say, unsure I want to hear her offer, but what the hell? I'm already here. And she did give me a rose, which I'll put in water as soon as I get back to my mom's apartment.

"If you come to one of our informational meet and greets, I'll consider making an appearance at Mickey's shower. How does that sound?"

"I'm flattered, Mrs. Esop. Really, I am. But between school, work, and my family life I already have a lot on my plate," I say, trying to get out of it. But judging from the way both she and Mickey are staring at me, I don't think I can get out of it.

"I'm sure you'll think about it and get back to me with the right answer," Mrs. Esop says, picking up her tools and placing them in the straw basket on the ground next to her feet. She looks up into the foyer and shakes her head at the sight of my friends heading up the stairs without me. I guess they're tired of waiting.

"Live your life, Jayd, not someone else's," she says. "Enjoy the rose."

"Thank you, and I'll definitely think about your suggestion." Satisfied, Mrs. Esop walks across her yard, heading to the garage to put her gardening supplies away before going in for the evening.

Me, a debutante? I can't even think about that right now. I don't think Mickey will be too happy to know that Mrs. Esop will only agree to come to the shower if I attend one of her sorority meetings. I'll leave out the details of the deal and just tell her that Mrs. Esop did agree to consider making an appearance. That should be enough to make her and Nickey Shantae happy for the time being. Maybe now I can enjoy the rest of the evening with my friends before it's time to call it a night.

"Drivers, start your engines," the male voice announces through the bullhorn. The crowd goes wild as we rev our engines. The spinning tires cause smoke to rise, making it hard to stay cool. I look straight ahead, ignoring the opponents on either side of me. I check out the leather interior and notice this car is familiar to me: I'm driving Jeremy's Mustang.

"Remember what I told you about the boost button, Jayd," Jeremy yells to me from the sidelines. "Push it when you

take her at the bend." Take who where? And why am I the one racing the hot rod? This is Jeremy's territory, not mine.

"You're going to lose," a girl's voice shouts from the car to my left. It's Sandy, with Rahima in the backseat. I'm grateful the baby's in her car seat, but her mama's still a fool for driving fast with her child in the car. Even in my dreams Sandy's actions are irrational.

"So are you," Trish, Rah's most recent ex-girlfriend, shouts to Sandy from the car on my right. "The prize is mine to take home."

"Ready, set, drive!" the announcer yells, and we're off. Sandy takes the lead and Trish is right behind her. We fly around the first leg of the lap, one car behind the other. I focus on the road ahead, letting them both think they've already got me beat. But slow and steady wins the race, and I'm secure in my pace.

"Jayd, catch up!" Rah yells from the finish line. He's seated up high on a pedestal, with a crown on his head like he's Mr. America. Is he the prize we're racing for?

After the first lap is complete the crowd's energy reaches an all-time high. Now I feel ready to show off what this car can really do. I glance to the right side of the speedometer, checking for the boost button just in case I need it. But I don't think it'll be necessary. These girls can't drive like I can.

I ease the car into fifth gear, pressing on the clutch so smoothly the car doesn't even jerk when the shift is complete. Then I put my foot to the floor, leaving both of my competitors in the dust.

"Yeah, Lady J. That's what I'm talking about, baby," Jeremy says, jumping up and down in the stands, he's so hyped. I love driving this car. I easily take the lead in the second lap as Trish and Sandy lag behind.

"All I have to do is finish this last lap and I can claim my prize," I say out loud. I continue driving, feeling the rush through my body as the night air hits me in the face through the open windows. I could drive at this speed all the time. There's something about the energy of controlling a fast car that makes me feel invincible. Feeling as indestructible as I do, Sandy gets right behind me, bumping my car with her bumper. What the hell?

"Get off my ass," I say into my rearview mirror. I know she can't hear me, but she can read my lips. "Back off now, Sandy, before someone gets hurt." Ignoring my warning, she bumps me again, this time causing me to slightly lose my grip on the steering wheel.

"I'm not going anywhere, Jayd. Rah's mine," she mouths back to me with a determined look in her eyes. Rahima looks scared to death in the backseat of her mother's car. If Sandy doesn't quit, she's liable to cause a spinout and that could kill us all.

"Push the button, Jayd," Jeremy shouts, reminding me that I have a secret weapon. I look at Sandy revving her engine, ready to hit me again. As she makes contact I push the button, propelling me full-throttle to the finish line. As I cross the line, I look in my rearview mirror and see Sandy's car spin out of control, causing Trish to run into her. When they finally stop spinning, both cars burst into flames.

"Rahima!" I yell, bringing my car to a full stop and running toward the flames. Rah jumps off his pedestal, hurting his leg as he hits the ground. In pain, he runs over to the car, freeing Rahima, but she's badly burned. Sandy and Trish also make it out but are both badly hurt.

"I told you to stop, Sandy, but as usual you don't listen," I say while checking on Rahima in her daddy's arms. Poor baby. Jeremy runs over to the tragic scene and hugs me

tightly. I look at Rah and his girls. They look at the fire, un-
fazed by their wounds. Am I the only one who thinks it's
time to stop this insanity? Rah is not a prize to be won, and
none of this is worth our lives—especially not Rahima's.

"You're not her mama, Jayd. I am and always will be,"
Sandy says, stating the obvious.

"*I'm a diva.*" Beyoncé snaps me out of my disturbing
dream and I am now wide-awake. I feel around the couch for
my phone. I was sleeping so wild that it's no longer in its customary place underneath my pillow.

"Hello," I say into my cell without checking the caller ID.

"Jayd, what's up with you?" Shawntrese's boyfriend, Leroy,
says. "You braiding today?" I prop myself up on my elbows
and rub the sleep from my eyes. What time is it, anyway?

"Yeah, after I get off work this afternoon." I'm leaving the
shop early today so I can catch up on my own clients' heads.

After last night's session was over, I came home and crashed
hard. My dream last night has been bothering me all day. I
texted Rah just to make sure they were okay. Usually my pre-
monitions come true in one way or another, and if it has anything to do with Rahima, I have to check it out.

Mama, Netta, and I really didn't have a chance to catch up
this afternoon. When I left a couple of hours ago, there were
still six clients in the shop. I made sure they were all out of
the washbowl and either under a dryer or in a chair before I
left. Netta has it under control, even if she likes to playfully
make me feel guilty for leaving early. I'm glad she's grown accustomed to having me around instead of handling all of her
clients alone, since Mama only works in the back of the shop.
I don't know how she did it, nor do I want to. Netta and Mama
let me into their prosperous world and I'm here to stay.

My own business is also doing well. My clientele has doubled in the past couple of months, and with summer around the corner, I know boys and girls alike are going to be sporting braids in some form or fashion. Not only is that good for my bank account, the variety will force me to up my game, and I'm looking forward to the challenge.

Speaking of challenges, Shawntrese's oily scalp is getting on my last nerve. I always schedule her appointments either first or last so I can spend as much time on her as possible. My neighbor's abused crown needs the most attention.

"It's confused, that's what it is," I say, carefully eyeing Shawntrese's scalp while looking around my mom's apartment at all of the cleaning I have left to do. "Maybe if you'd stop treating it like a stepchild and love it like your own, it'll know how to act." This is the most unpredictable head of hair I've ever encountered. It's dry as sandpaper one day and as greasy as bacon the next.

"Aren't you supposed to bring positive energy to my hair?" Shawntrese says, mocking my motto. I don't care what she says; this girl knows her head needs some serious love. My cell vibrates on the table and with my hands slick from braiding I can't pick it up.

"Shawntrese, open that for me, please," I say. Shawntrese props the open phone between my right shoulder and ear without looking up from *Chappelle's Show* reruns on the television. I usually don't answer unidentified calls, but it might be money. So far word of mouth has been my best promoter.

"What up, Jayd?" Sandy says. What the hell is she doing calling me, and on a Saturday night? Wherever she's calling from is loud in the background. I hope she's not in jail again. And how did she get my number?

"What's up?" I ask, adjusting Shawntrese's head to form the perfect braid. I'm glad she doesn't remember me burning out a patch of her delicate hair when I had my sleep-walking issues a couple of weeks ago because Mama, my mom and I made sure it never happened, just like all of Misty's mess. She also doesn't remember how vexed she was, but I do. And I never want to see that side of my neighbor and loyal customer again.

"I need you to come get Rahima and take her home for me. Rah will meet you there in a little while," she says, like I'm the nanny. What the hell?

"Did you call the right number?" I ask, finishing up the last row in Shawntrese's head. I wipe my hands on her towel, hand her the mirror from the dining room table and gener-ously spray my lavender and eucalyptus braid sheen over my immaculate creation. Shawntrese runs her hand over her tightly woven scalp and smiles, obviously pleased with the finished product.

"Yes, I called the right number, Jayd. Stop playing and come get this little girl. I've got to be on stage in a half hour and Carla is already working. Like I said, Rah will meet you at the house."

"Sandy, have you lost your mind? I'm not the sitter and I'm working myself," I say, taking Shawntrese's twenty-dollar bill and tucking it into my bra for safekeeping. Mama says if I put my money there first I'll always have more money to come. It may sound like a silly superstition to some, but it's working for me.

"Jayd, this is serious. Rahima can't be at the club for much longer, and I've got to get this paper. Besides, I thought you wanted to play the mama anyway. Here's your chance," she says sourly. Did Sandy say her two-year-old daughter is at the club?

"You've got the baby at a strip joint, Sandy?" I yell into the phone. Shawntrese looks at me in shock, soaking up all the details to dish to the neighbors later. This trick Sandy has completely lost her mind. And I thought I was irresponsible when I left Rahima sleeping upstairs while I sleepwalked down the stairs. But that's nothing compared to purposely taking the baby to a place where people get shot and stabbed on the regular.

"Duh, Jayd. That's why I'm calling you. Rah had to go to Compton and drop Kamal off at their grandparents' house before handling some business on that side of town. I called him already and he ain't answering the phone. So can you come get her or not?"

"What'd she say?" Shawntrese asks, noticing the frown on my face. How do I explain that my friend's baby is at a strip joint where her grandmother and mother work and that I feel obligated to go get this child? This is some ghetto bull, for real.

"Jayd, are you there?" I don't know how to respond. How could she take Rahima to a place like that, and then ask her baby-daddy's ex-girlfriend to come and get her baby? "Look, I've got to change Rahima's diaper. Text me when you get here and I'll have one of the other girls let you back here. Bye," Sandy says, hanging up before I have a chance to reply. She knows how much I love that little girl and uses it to her advantage every time. I just met Rahima a few months ago, but—much like Mickey's unborn child—my sense of responsibility for her is strong.

"Shawntrese, you will not believe where I have to go," I say, heading to the bathroom to wash my hands. I'm working hard trying to repair the years of perm damage in Shawntrese's hair and it seems to be paying off. But her scalp is still hella oily and always leaves my hands extra shiny. I would normally take a shower after my last client leaves, but that'll have to wait until I get back tonight.

"I heard," she says. I walk back into the living room and

dust myself off. I've got hair all over me. "You want me to come with you?" Shawntrese asks, taking the towel from around her shoulders and standing up. She stretches her thin arms like a cat, and I catch a glimpse of the new tattoo on her belly. I hope she and Leroy work out now that she has his name written on her body for the world to see. Sandy did that with Rah and we see where they've ended up. My hands still feel greasy. Damn this girl's oily scalp. I need to wash my hands one more time before I leave.

"Would you, please?" I say from the bathroom. "I have no business going up in that club by myself," I say, drying my hands. I walk back into the living room and check the rest of the apartment before retrieving my purse from the coatrack. I take my keys out, ready to roll.

"Sure I will. My boo is a regular at The Pimp Palace. They know me up there," Shawntrese says as I slip on my sandals and grab my jacket off the coatrack. It's a warm night, but I'll take my jacket just in case.

"How did you know that's where Sandy works?" I ask, opening the multiple locks on my mom's front door. Shawntrese walks out ahead of me and down the stairs while I relock the door.

"Because she's one of Leroy's favorite new dancers. Rah's mama, Carla, is on his list, too." I look at Shawntrese and don't know what to say. I'm embarrassed that she knows Rah's baby-mama and Carla from the club, but more embarrassed that she didn't tell me—even though I can understand why. It's not a typical topic of conversation you have with your girl.

"I see," I say, leading the way down the long driveway toward the parking lot. Never would I have imagined that I'd be driving my mom's car to a strip club, but here goes nothing. Wait until she finds out about this one. I'm surprised my mom hasn't checked in yet. She and her man, Karl, must be

too busy for her to get caught up in my never-ending tragedy
with Rah.

When we arrive at The Pimp Palace, there are cars wrapped
around the corner trying to get into the lot. The sign above
the entrance says TWENTY-DOLLAR PARKING. I'll be damned if I
spend my hard-earned money like that. Noticing my scoping
eyes, Shawntrese points to an empty spot across the street.
We look at each other and shrug our shoulders at the risky
spot. This is not the best neighborhood to be in, especially not
two young women alone at night. If I have anything to say
about it, this will be a quick trip.

"I feel you wanting to save money, but it's not the best
idea to park outside of the lot," Shawntrese says as I carefully
maneuver the compact vehicle into the tight space. Parallel
parking with a clutch is tricky, but I think I'm finally getting
the hang of it. I feel her, too, but this shit isn't worth twenty
of my dollars.

"The radio's already gone and there's nothing else to
steal," I say, turning the engine off, unlocking the doors and
exiting the little ride. Shawntrese gets out and walks around
to where I'm standing near the curb.

"What about the car?" she asks, looking both ways before
crossing the busy intersection. Jaywalking is a serious viola-
tion in Los Angeles, and a dangerous one at that. Most drivers
don't seem to have any sympathy for people who choose to
walk outside of the designated pedestrian area, including us.

"I doubt anyone will steal the whip," I say, running across
the intersection and joining her on the other side.

The Pimp Palace takes up the majority of the corner. Other
small stores nearby are closed for the evening. The ballers
are out tonight and apparently ready to spend money. The
parking lot is full, with many more cars waiting in line to get

in. The sign on the door also reads TWENTY DOLLARS PER PERSON. By the time you get up in the spot you've already spent forty dollars. I wonder how much the clients spend on the girls?

"Try not to look too pretty, Jayd. They might think you're here to work," Shawntrese says, touching her braids. "I'm already too flyy to do anything about it." She is so crazy. I reach inside my purse and send Sandy a one-word text letting her know I'm here. I'm going to kill Rah when I see him for letting this heffa back in our lives.

Shawntrese leads the way to the front door and informs the hostess seated at the table that we're here to see Sandy. The girl looks us over and then asks us to open our purses for a weapons check.

"Do you have any knives, guns, pepper spray?" the hostess asks, meddling through my junky Lucky Brand bag. I'm slightly embarrassed at the state of disarray the purse is in. There's a big-ass dude posted behind the hostess, watching her feel us up. I guess he checks the dudes out and watches the girls.

"No, I don't. Do I need some?" I ask. Shawntrese laughs as the hostess checks her next. I know she thinks I'm being a smart-ass, but I'm serious. I don't know what to take when frequenting a spot like this. Once we're all clear, the male guard lets us through the black velvet curtain separating the waiting area from the inside of the club.

Girls. Everywhere I look there are barely dressed girls who look about my age, dancing or walking around. There are other women who look slightly older, but none over thirty. I wonder how old Rah's mom—Carla—pretends to be?

"Sandy's downstairs in the locker room," the same hostess says, pointing at the door to our left. "You'll have to pay if you want to see the show."

"We're good," Shawntrese says, pulling my arm toward the door. I'm glad she's here because I think I'm in a state of shock. How can Sandy and Carla work like this? And how can the supposed gatekeepers just let my sixteen-year-old self walk up in here, no ID or anything? I hope it's only because Sandy said something, and not their normal mode of operation.

"Jayd, are you okay?" Shawntrese asks, holding on to my arm and guiding me down the stairs. What little fresh air we had in the waiting area has been replaced by a thick funk. I look at the girls passing us by in the stairwell and notice that some of them look younger than I do. I wonder how many of them are mamas already.

"Are you girls here for the job?" another male security guard says to us as we approach the locker room at the bottom of the stairs. The stench down here is worse than the smell in the school locker room after gym class.

"Say what?" I automatically reply. "Do I look like a stripper?" I ask, completely offended. I'm wearing my hip-hugger sweats, a T-shirt and the yellow bebe sandals Jeremy bought me months ago. Shawntrese is dressed in a Nike sweat suit. Neither of us looks ready for an audition.

"No," Shawntrese says, taking over the conversation before I go completely off. "We're here to see Sandy." I look around and notice the dancers watching us like the fresh meat that we are. I am totally out of my element and they know it.

"Oh, y'all must be here to pick up that baby," the guard says, suddenly less interested in us, and I'm glad for it. "She's back there." He gestures behind us toward the locker room and returns to reading his newspaper. Behind his post is an exit sign and the only other way out of the building from what I can see. The locker room takes up the rest of the stuffy space.

"Sandy," I say, entering the locker room while trying to ignore the loud women all around us prepping for the stage. This is nothing like opening night of any play I've ever performed in.

"Hi, Jayd," Rahima says, smiling up at me as I pick her up from the chair she's seated in. She smells fresh, like baby powder and Desitin. I told Rah to stop putting that diaper rash cream on her and start potty training the girl. But I can't give her mother the same advice, no matter how right I may be. I'm not the mama and I'm reminded of it every time Sandy's around.

"Hey, baby girl. You ready to go home?" I ask, picking up her diaper bag with my free hand while Shawntrese claims her car seat, ready to go. I don't know how Mickey's going to manage all the stuff babies come with, with her long nails—I almost broke one just now, and my nails are nowhere near as long as the claws my girl sports.

"She already ate dinner," Sandy says off the rip. No hello, no thank-you—nothing. This trick's got her nerve and then some. Shawntrese looks at me and then at Sandy, rolling her eyes hard. I would've told Sandy off by now, but I'm trying to stay cool for Rahima's sake.

"You're welcome," I say with much attitude. I hope she doesn't mistake my kindness for weakness, because I will check her ass in a minute if it has to go down like that.

"Oh, please, Jayd. You ain't doing this for me or my daughter. You're doing this for Rah," she says, sucking her teeth and wiping her brow with her arm. The way she's sweating she must've just come off-stage. There's cash sticking out of every possible place it can on a woman. Rather than stand here arguing with this broad, I follow Shawntrese out, but not before I claim some reimbursement for my time. I reach for a twenty-dollar bill hanging out of the garter around Sandy's left arm and snatch it from its holding place.

"This is for parking," I say, turning around to head back out of the stuffy room and up the stairs before she can protest. Rah's going to hear about this when I see him tonight. This is not how I get down at all, and he knows it.

I send Rah a text telling him to meet me back at his house and he dutifully replies. I'm sure he's retrieved all his messages by now. If picking children up from strip clubs at night is the way he's living nowadays, I'm definitely out of the equation. Last night's dream about racing for him was yet another warning about what will happen if I keep dealing with Rah and his broads. And I've got too much work to do to deal with this shit on the regular.

"Jayd, what are you doing, picking up Rah's baby from a strip club? Girl, what's the matter with you? I told you Rahima's not your responsibility," my mom yells into my head as we cross the busy intersection. I guess she's not too busy to check in on me after all. I feel special, but her anger isn't helping my concentration. The last thing I need is a distraction with this thick toddler on my hip.

"I couldn't just leave her there," I think back, unlocking the car doors with the remote. I step onto the curb while Shawntrese puts the car seat securely in the backseat. I don't know what they've been feeding this girl, but she's getting heavy.

"The hell you couldn't. No matter how much you may love Rah, you're not married to that little boy. Stop acting like it." As usual, my mom's right. The last time I babysat Rahima, her daddy stayed out all night long, leaving me to dream some crazy shit about being his next baby-mama. That wasn't a good feeling. And by acting like Rahima's stepmother I'm taking on all of the responsibilities of being a mother without the respect of being a girlfriend first. This bull will end tonight.

* * *

By the time I drop Shawntrese off at home, Rahima's fast asleep. It's been a long night for all of us. I hope Rah gets here soon, because I want to pass out, too. There's a car parked in Rah's driveway, but it's not his Acura. Pulling into the driveway, I can clearly see Trish's car.

"What the hell are you doing here?" I ask Trish, pulling up next to her and turning off the car. I look back at Rahima, who looks so peaceful. I hate to take her out of the car. Only her daddy knows how to keep her asleep while in transport.

"I'm here to watch Rahima. Sandy sent me a text saying she was being dropped off and there was no one here, so I came," she says as Rah pulls up behind me. His look of sheer surprise can only mean one thing: Sandy set us all up. What an expert bitch move. I give Nellie my blessing if she wants to greet Sandy as a bitch all day long.

"That was really sweet of you, Trish. But as you can see, we've got it all under control," I say, exiting my mom's car and gently closing the door.

"I'll wait for her daddy to tell me I'm not needed, if it's all the same to you." I look at Trish's blank expression as she steps out of her Accord and feel sorry for her bland ass. She really thinks she can stay in Rah's life by being his call girl—the chick he can call on when he needs money, a sitter, and anything else she can give. Doesn't she know that guys get tired of having their desires met that easily?

"Hey, what's going on here?" Rah asks, peeking through the back window of my ride and checking on his daughter like the good daddy he is—most of the time.

"Sandy asked me to be here when Rahima got here because no one was home and you both had to work," Trish says, walking up to Rah and giving him a hug. He pats her on the back and looks at me uncomfortably. This is exactly why he can never say shit to me about my relationship with Jeremy.

No matter what he says about them just being friends, he's always got Trish on the side. Trish misses Rah, and if it weren't for his connection to her brother, she'd have no excuse to be at his house all the time. Sandy calls her just to vex me, and Trish is probably clueless that she's being played by Sandy.

"I'm sorry Sandy dragged you into this, but Jayd's got Rahima and I'm in for the night," he says, backing away from Trish and returning to my ride to get his baby girl out of the backseat. I reach through the open window and grab the diaper bag. Why isn't Trish moving?

"I'm not leaving until I hear from Sandy," Trish says, locking her car and walking toward the front door. If she's listening to anything Sandy's got to say, this girl is crazier than I thought. Instead of telling her to hit the road, Rah agrees to let her wait in the house. Am I the only one who sees this is insane? I can't take anymore of this twisted reality. I follow them into the house and back to Rah's bedroom where he lays his daughter down on his bed without disturbing her. I'm impressed with the way he handles Rahima. The way he treats me is the problem I'm having.

"Rah, who am I to you, for real? Because you come at me like I'm your girl, but we all know that's not true. And as much as I love Rahima, I'm not her mama. Trish has more of a say in her life than I do." Rah looks at me, putting his finger up for me to lower my voice.

"Jayd, that's not true," he says, leading me into Kamal's bedroom next door to his and closing the door. This is the first conversation we've had in a week, and just like the last time we spoke, we're arguing. "I know that picking up Rahima from Sandy's job was a bit much, but you came through, baby. And I appreciate you," he says, putting his arms around my waist and pulling me in close to him.

"Trish is in the living room, in case you forgot," I say, pushing him away. "And this isn't a competition. I couldn't care less how much you appreciate me dealing with your shit. Do you appreciate me for who I am, not for what I can do for you? That's the question."

"Jayd, you know I need you in my life. Yes, I appreciate you for you. You're my best friend," he says, trying to kiss me, but the last thing I want is Rah touching me. I don't care how good his chiseled chocolate arms look popping out of his Adidas T-shirt. This brotha's not getting any love from me tonight.

"Yes, and Sandy's the one you live with, and Trish is the one you sleep with. I got the roles down in my head," I say, walking toward the door. Rah steps in front of me, blocking my way. I look up into his dark brown eyes and wish we could go back to the two twelve-year-olds in love we were over four years ago. But we can't go back there and I don't know where we're headed.

"You're the one I love, girl. You know that," he says, not denying Sandy and Trish's functions in his life. He could've at least said he wasn't sleeping with Trish, but I guess he didn't want to get caught in a lie. That's as good as a confession to me.

"You can have your love, because from where I'm standing it's highly overrated," I say, pushing Rah out of my way and opening the bedroom door. I walk down the hallway and into the living room where Trish is seemingly posted up for the night. Sandy's busy shaking her ass at work and won't get to her cell for a while.

"Jayd, please stay," Rah calls after me. "We can work this out." I can't take it anymore. My head is pounding and it's late. Trish can buy into this tired-ass Jerry Springer family drama if she wants to. I clean my hands of the whole mess.

Saving Rahima from having another crazy-ass teenage parental figure in her life is the most important thing I can do for that little girl. And I can only do that by first saving myself.

~ 7 ~
Survivors

*"Can only sing the words/
It's up to you to listen."*

—ANGIE STONE

By the time I got back to my mom's apartment last night, all I had the energy to do was take a much-needed shower and pass out on the couch. I look down at my cell and see that I've missed fifteen calls, all of which are from Rah, I assume. My growling stomach urges me to get up from my makeshift bed and walk into the kitchen to see what I can whip up for breakfast, but not before I wash my face.

On the way into the bathroom I hear someone walking up the stairs outside the apartment. It had better not be another pop-up visit from Jeremy.

"Jayd, unlock the chain," my mom says through the door. How come she didn't give a sistah a heads-up she was coming home? The place is a mess, and I don't want to hear her mouth about it.

"Fancy seeing you here this morning," I say, unlocking the door and letting her into her own apartment. My mom kisses me on the cheek, kicks off her sandals, and speed-walks to her bedroom. She must've run out of clothes at Karl's house and came home to restock.

"How's your weekend going, other than frequenting a strip club?" my mom asks, dumping her overnight bag full of dirty clothes on the floor to make space for clean ones. She needs to do her laundry.

"It's going cool. I made a lot of money and got to drive Chance's car on Friday. That was the highlight," I say, sitting on the corner of her bed. I love it when my mom's home. Ever since she and Karl started dating I rarely spend any time with her. I'm not hating, but I think she should fit me into her schedule. We only have the weekends together and I'm lucky if I get to see her at all.

"Chance has the Chevy, right?" my mom says, quickly sifting through hangers and tossing dresses onto the bed next to me. I need to start taking advantage of her closet more often.

"Yes, and it's so nice to drive." I can feel the engine purring just thinking about it.

"And fast," my mom says, her green eyes sparkling. "I had a boyfriend with one of those. I was hot shit when I would drive that car. Feels good, huh?" my mom asks, smiling at her memory.

"It sure does. I can't wait to get behind the wheel again," I say. I'm flattered that Chance trusts me to drive his classic vehicle. He's spent a lot of time and money on his car, and it's worth every ounce of both. He and Jeremy like to work on cars, but it's not a passion like it is with Rah and Nigel, who fix up cars like they ball: constantly. Jeremy and Chance know a lot of people who they pay to do the work that Nigel and Rah do simply for the love of it. Either way, they all have nice rides.

"You're only young once, Jayd. I say live it up." I agree with my mom. I plan on driving all of Jeremy's friends' cars and Rah's people, too. Whoever lets me behind the wheel—I'm going for it. I also want to drive Jeremy's Mustang. Although I'm no expert, I think Jeremy's car is faster than Chance's.

My phone vibrates in my hand and I see a text message from Rah. My stomach growls, reminding me that I still need to eat. Maybe Trish can make him breakfast this morning, because I know the broad is still there.

> Hey, baby. I'm sorry about last night. And I promise I'm not doing anything with Trish. She left right after you did. I'll give you some time to cool off, but please call me. I love you.

I told Rah what he could do with his love last night, and I meant it.

"Oh, no. What's wrong now? Or should I say what did Rah do this time?" my mom asks, moving on to her underwear drawer.

"It's just the usual insanity that is Rah's life," I say, erasing the text and closing the phone. My mom zips her bag shut and sits down next to me for a moment before we both start our day.

"Jayd, what is it about Rah that keeps you holding on to him no matter how unhealthy the situation becomes? And don't say that baby, because I will scream in your head if you do." I know my mom's serious if she's threatening to hurt me on a psychic level.

"I don't know how to answer that," I say, thinking about her question. Is there anything good about us other than our long friendship?

"I'm glad you're being honest," she says, taking the overnight bag and putting it on her lap. "Think about it seriously, Jayd, and then make a list of all the good versus the bad. If the good outweighs the bad, then stick it out. But if the negative side of the list is longer, then you need to get out before it's too late." My mom looks into my eyes and smiles before kissing me good-bye.

"Thank you, Mom," I say, rising from the bed so I can lock the door behind her. She's given me something to think about. And I like the idea of making a list, although I'm afraid I already know how it's going to turn out. And what if Rah's negatives do outweigh his positives? What do I do then?

"You take care of Jayd. And don't feel a bit of guilt about looking out for your own survival. That's a huge part of why we're here, baby," my mom says without moving her lips, even though she's within speaking range.

"I hear you loud and clear," I say, giving her a hug before she's gone. I only have two customers this morning and the rest of the day is mine to catch up on school and spirit work— no boys and their craziness allowed.

After braiding two heads and last night's dramatic state of affairs, I'm ready to chill for the rest of the afternoon until I have to go back to Compton. Being at the beach always makes me feel better. I figured the water would give me the serenity I need to clear my head. I could run after Rahima all afternoon, clean house, and braid five heads in a row and still have more energy than I do after an encounter with Sandy. And recently, dealing with Rah has been no better.

Love sucks. That's all I have to say about that subject, for real. I really don't see the point of having a boyfriend. All that the boys in my life do is create misery. They either bring me drama or some female in their life does the honors for them. But I love them, I really do. When I'm not talking to Rah I feel incomplete. For the two years we didn't talk after I found out he got Sandy pregnant, I always thought about him. The whole reason I was attracted to KJ in the first place was because he was the closest thing I could get to Rah at school. And KJ was no match for the real thing.

It's time for me to let the past go. I love Rah, but I can't let him drag me off my chosen path. And as for Jeremy, I haven't had too many dreams about him. And whenever he is in a dream he's usually catching me, or trying to save me in some other way. I'm feeling Jeremy strongly, but I don't love him like I love Rah. I don't know if I can ever fully shake Rah from my system, or if I really want to. When I'm ready, I know I can find something in the spirit book to help, which is at Mama's house where it always is.

My mom's incomplete spirit notebook has some good suggestions in it, too. I brought it with me to study while enjoying the seawater and sun. I wish I could do this every weekend, but I don't have that kind of time. This book looks and smells like it's been around for centuries. I'm glad we have a written account of the multiple paths in our lineage, at least for the most part. Since my mom stopped keeping up with her notes and recording the notes about her mother's path, those sections are deficient. But I'm doing my best to keep up with what I can now. I keep pretty good notes in my spirit notebook and will transfer them to the family spirit book after my initiation.

I'm not ready to become anyone's wife yet, which is what you spiritually become to your orisha, once initiated. I'm not ready to be Oshune's wife, or Rah's wifey and Rahima's step-mama. Technically, I guess I would be a step-girl, because I'm not married to her daddy. Hell, we're not even boyfriend and girlfriend at the moment. Trish and Jeremy's presence in my life reminds me of that constantly. I think if I got Rah out of my system I could give Jeremy a real chance at being my man. I know what Mr. A said about dating a white boy, and he's right. Being in an interracial relationship has all kinds of challenges. But I like him—a lot—and after the way he reacted to Emilio kissing me, I know Jeremy's feeling me hard, too.

If I can give Rah a million chances after he's acted like an ass in more ways than one, I can give Jeremy a break after only a couple of major infractions. If Jeremy weren't white this would be a no-brainer. But because we have the added history of our great-ancestors being lovers per one of my dreams, the shit's just that much more complicated for me. I don't need anyone to tell me I'm in for it if I choose to date Jeremy exclusively.

The kind of black love that Nigel and Mickey found with each other is rare at our age. And my mom and Karl's relationship is a phenomenon if I ever saw one. The kind of love I usually witness is the torture that is Mama and Daddy's marriage. And to be honest, I think that's where most couples' relationships are headed, no matter how in love they are. Mama and Daddy used to be in puppy love with each other at first. But then reality set in and the sacrifices became apparent, each feeling undervalued in his or her own way, after giving up so much of themselves for so long. And that's the kind of love I feel Rah and I are in: that quicksand kind of love.

We've put so much into this relationship for the past four years, that neither of us is willing to give up on it now. But I've just about had it because—like quicksand—the harder you fight the faster you sink. I guess it's a good thing that I don't I have anymore fight left in me.

"What are you over here thinking about so seriously?" Jeremy asks, catching me in mid thought. Where did he come from and why didn't I hear him walk up?

"Life," I say, reaching up to meet his embrace halfway. He never officially apologized for calling me a tease. I know he didn't mean it, but we will have to eventually address it. But now is not the time. I can only deal with one issue at a time. "What are you doing here? I thought Redondo was your beach?"

"It's all my coastline," he says, stretching his arms out toward the ocean.

"Okay, Columbus," I say as he sits down in the sand next

to me. I love the way the warm sand feels in between my toes. Judging by the way Jeremy's playing in the sand with his hairy feet I'd say he feels the same way.

"Very funny, Lady J. There were too many tourists at the pier so I opted for a quieter, Manhattan Sunday." And I'm glad he did. Jeremy's energy is very soothing when he's calm. And I like being around him always. "I was just about to grab something to eat if you want to join me," he says, stroking my right arm with the back of his hand. I nod in agreement and he stands up, blocking the sun with his tall frame.

"Let me take you to lunch for a change," I say, taking Jeremy's hand as he reaches down to help me up. I brush the sand from my backside and Jeremy watches my every move. "Why don't you take a picture? It'll last longer," I say, walking ahead of him.

"I just might do that," he says, following me from the beach toward my car. The alarm on the brand-new Mercedes parked in front of my mom's car beeps and the engine starts. Who did that and can we be friends? I get closer to the black-on-black sports car and take a peek inside. It looks like something Batman would drive. SL 63 AMG. I don't know what any of that means, but I want one.

"Do you like it?" Jeremy asks, walking around the vehicle, also scoping the perfection before our eyes. This thing must've cost a grip.

"Like it?" I ask, following him around the vehicle. "I'm ready to make a long-term commitment to it." I stop and look at my reflection in the dark, tinted windows with Jeremy right behind me, staring into my eyes. We are opposites, but we look good together and feel even better.

"Get in," he says, opening the driver's door.

"Damn, Jeremy. Y'all got it like this?" I ask. I shouldn't be surprised. His entire block could have their own fleet of luxury vehicles. But to get a teenager these kinds of wheels is extreme, even for Jeremy's wealthy family.

"I wish," he says. I think that's the first time I've heard him openly express envy. Good to know he wants for something. "It belongs to a friend of mine. He went away for the weekend and let me babysit her. Sweet, huh?" he says, caressing the black leather seats with his hands like he did me a few moments ago. I glide into the seat, positioning myself under the steering wheel—my favorite part of the car. I'd love to drive this thing.

"Let's go," he says, closing the door and walking around to the other side. I didn't even have to ask and my wish came true. "Push the button and we can go," Jeremy says, buckling his seat belt. That's what he said in my dream when I drove his car in a race with Sandy and Trish. This must be a sign that I'm going the right way with Jeremy.

"I've got the perfect place to have lunch," I say, turning on the left blinker and approaching the traffic light. "Let's go to Simply Wholesome. You like their food and I would love a turkey burger," I say, heading toward my mom's neck of the woods. I don't mind driving back out that way since it's not my gas. And I'm going to take the long way down La Cienega Boulevard to get there. I want to savor this experience for as long as I can.

"Didn't you leave there on bad terms?" Jeremy asks, remembering the drama behind my career change a few months ago. He has a great memory for a self-proclaimed pothead.

"That's not the point," I say, gunning the engine hard down Aviation Boulevard. I feel like a rock star in this Benz. Jeremy's got some good friends, because if this were my car, I wouldn't let anyone drive it. "They have good food." And it's where everyone meets up to show off his or her bodies and cars. It's an LA thing: Jeremy's from the beach and can't relate.

"You're driving, Jayd. I'm just along for the ride and loving the view," Jeremy says, pulling his sunshades over his eyes and sitting back in his seat. His long legs barely fit in the cozy car, but I fit just right. "As long as you're this sexy behind the wheel, I'll go wherever you want me to." I never noticed how tight Jeremy's game is before. He's fine, got money, intelligent, kind, and he likes him some Jayd. So far, that's a pretty positive list.

When we get to Simply Wholesome the parking lot is packed, which is typical for a sunny Sunday afternoon. The cruisers are out today, their shiny cars still clean from a weekend wash and wax. It's a ritual for most people on this side of Los Angeles to hit up Crenshaw Car Wash on Saturdays so that their rides will be fresh for the rest of the weekend. I keep saying I'm going to take my mom's ride over there one day and let them work their magic, but I can't see spending fifteen of my hard-earned dollars getting the car washed, when I could pay one of my uncles five dollars to get the job done.

I find a parking spot on the side of the building and pull into the small space, causing heads to turn as I shut off the engine. I love driving this car, and it's the perfect day for it. We both get out and head to the restaurant side of the building, passing several customers hanging out and enjoying the nice weather and good food. I miss working here but I don't miss working with the shift manager, Marty.

"Damn, that's a sweet ride," Jeremy says, checking out Shakir's flawless Jaguar parked in front of the main entrance, as usual. I'm surprised Shakir doesn't have a permanent sign that says "reserved for owner" in his customary space, not that he needs it. Everyone knows the Jag belongs there.

"You act like you've never seen his ride before," I say, walking through the open double doors. The scent of coconut shakes and sweet-potato fries welcomes us in. I miss the vibe in this place and so does my stomach.

"If I have, I never noticed it," Jeremy says, still stuck on the black luxury automobile. Shakir, the owner, loves that car more than he loves Summer—the supervising manager and love of his life. "There's something different about it, I'm sure."

"It's the new set of twenty-twos I just purchased," Shakir says, smiling at Jeremy as he gives me a big hug. His locks have grown, but I can tell no one's keeping them up for him. Maybe I should offer him my services.

"I knew it," Jeremy says, like an excited two-year-old boy. What is it with dudes and cars? I return Shakir's warm embrace, glad he's happy to see me. I've missed working here, and he's always been good to me. My mom hasn't been up here since I quit, but I know she and Shakir still keep in touch. They went to high school together and will always be friends, just like Rah and me.

"It's good to see you, Jayd. It's been a long time," Shakir says, letting me go to shake Jeremy's hand.

"Jeremy, this is Shakir, the owner of Simply Wholesome and my former boss. Shakir, this is my friend Jeremy," I say. Although Jeremy picked me up from work several times he never came in and met the crew.

"Ah, the infamous Jeremy," Shakir says, making me blush. When I worked here Jeremy was all I could talk about, just like I used to talk about Rah, who is a regular up here because his house is right up the street. Rah was probably more distraught over me quitting than I was. We both hate that there's no more discounted healthy food. The menu prices are pretty steep, but well worth it. "It's nice to meet you, man."

"Likewise," Jeremy says, refocusing his attention on the Jaguar. Are we ever going to make it all the way inside the restaurant? I'm hungry, and the smell of the food is working my senses overtime. Everything is made fresh to order, and I need them to get on my turkey burger and black beans, stat.

"Do you want to take a look inside?" Shakir asks Jeremy, taking out his keys and pointing the remote at the vehicle. Not only does Shakir turn off the alarm, but he also starts the car, rolls down the windows, and starts the music, causing all heads in- and outside of his business to turn. Men and their toys.

"Oh hell, yes," Jeremy says, mesmerized by the car. We just got out of a vehicle that makes this one look like yesterday's news, yet Jeremy's salivating all over the onyx cat. I guess dudes can never have too many pretty things. If it were a woman, I'm sure he'd have no problem leaving me for the chance to be with her. "You don't mind, do you, Jayd?" Oh, now he remembers that I'm here.

"Not at all. As long as you don't mind me eating without you," I say, giving him a big smile. He's so cute when he's excited about something that I can't be mad at him for too long.

"Yeah, of course. I'll take whatever you're having," he says, reaching into his jean pocket and pulling out a twenty.

"It's on me, remember?" I say, putting my hand up in protest. "I got this, man." Jeremy bends down and kisses me on my nose.

"Thank you," he says before following Shakir to his car. It feels nice to be able to do something for Jeremy. After all, he's always so generous with me now that we've established that I can't be bought. It's nice to be able to treat him for a change.

I walk through the front door, almost running into one of the three palm trees next to the customer bench where people usually wait for takeout orders. When did the trees get this big?

"Jayd," Sarah, my former coworker, says, scaring the hell out of me. I've missed her loud Jamaican ass. She runs around the counter to give me a hug, damn the long line of customers at the register. "My girl!"

"What's up, Miss Sarah? How have you been?" I glance around the restaurant and see nothing much has changed. Summer walks in from the business office across from where we're standing and smiles my way. It feels nice to be missed.

"I've been good, girl. Except we're still working under Satan's daughter, but it's not as bad as it was before," she says, getting back to work before someone says something. The customers may be bougie, but they're still black and will get ghetto if need be.

I take my place at the end of the long line like everyone else. I wish I were still employed here, if only because I could walk to the back and put my order in myself instead of waiting behind all the other customers. I also wouldn't mind receiving the thirty-percent employee discount.

Sarah works at one register while Marty controls the other. Alonzo nods "what's up" to me from the juice bar behind the registers he's got under control this afternoon. As luck would have it, Marty's register frees up first when I finally make it to the counter, forcing me to place my order with her. But before I can give her my request, I notice her dandruff-ridden shirt. This woman needs my help and doesn't even know it.

"You know, my grandmother makes something for that," I say, watching Marty dust the dandruff off her shoulders, which is even more apparent because of her black shirt. I look up at her hair and see the large white patches all over her scalp. She must've been scratching it all day. Poor thing. I can't help but want to heal her head.

"That's okay. I've got it under control." Whatever. If the trick doesn't want my help it's her loss. She's such a hater she can't even tell when someone's being genuinely nice to her. As a hairdresser I hate to see people suffering needlessly when we have the tools to make their lives better. Marty unconsciously scratches her scalp, releasing even more flakes onto her shirt. I can't take it anymore. It's grossing out me and the other customers in line. I look over at Sarah, who sucks her teeth in disdain.

"Marty, for real. The line of products will work wonders on your scalp and hair. If you don't believe me, I can give you a sample to test." She looks at me angrily. I don't know if it's because her involuntary snowflakes embarrass her or because she just hates me that much. But whatever the reason, I know she needs my help. "I think I may have some in my purse," I say, sifting through my bag.

"Why do you care?" Marty's got a point there. Why *do* I care? I'm willing to give this heffa some of my own personal supply and she's such a hater she probably won't even use it. How can she be so proud and stupid at the same time?

"Never mind," I say, rolling my eyes and placing my order. Marty takes my money and gives me my number. I hope she doesn't think she's getting another tip. Good hair advice is just as valuable as money, and she threw it back in my face. "Thank you," I say as I step to the side of the counter near the store entrance and wait for our food.

"Jayd," I hear Rah say as he walks in from the store side of the establishment with Rahima on his hip. Damn, this is not happening again. Why are he and Jeremy always in the same space at the same time, with me caught in the middle? I haven't spoken to him since I left his house last night, and haven't answered any of his messages today either. I'm still steaming from our encounter with Trish and the fact that I had to pick up his child from a strip club.

"Hi, Rahima, Rah," I say, smiling at his daughter. Before we can get into it, our eyes instinctively follow a girl and a guy who look out of place in the restaurant, wearing dark clothes and baseball hats. Rah and I look around the restaurant and store, following the two strangers' gazes before returning our focus to each other. We both acknowledge the similar feeling that the place is being scoped for a robbery, and try to shake it off for the time being.

"I'm glad to see you made it home safely last night," Rah says sourly.

"Did Trish?" I ask. His brown eyes narrow in annoyance as he tries to think of a response. What can he say? Rah has no right to talk shit to me about anything and besides, this is not the time or the place. Sunday is the day he usually works on cars and I've got a lunch date.

"Babe, thanks for being patient with me," Jeremy says, putting his arm around my shoulders before noticing my companions. "Hey, what's up, man?" Jeremy says to Rah who returns the greeting with a nod. I look at Rahima, who looks like she could use some sleep.

"You need a nap, sweetie?" I ask Rahima. She reaches her arms out for me to take her. I can't resist, and claim her from her daddy. Jeremy looks at the scene and I realize he's never met Rah's daughter.

"Rahima, this is my friend Jeremy," I say, making the formal introduction. Rah looks like he's about to bust a blood vessel he's so jealous. Oh well. If he'd learned how to act maybe our relationship would have survived. But he poisoned it when he invited Sandy in.

"She's a cutie," Jeremy says, looking down at Rahima's sleepy eyes. Jeremy's own baby will be born in the next couple of months. He doesn't like to talk about it, but I know his ex-girlfriend Tania's running off with his unborn child to get married in New York has to bother him a little.

"Number forty-six," Marty calls from her register. I can tell she wants to scratch her head even though she's trying to control the urge. I hope she changes her mind about using Mama's products.

"That's us," I say, kissing Rahima on the forehead and

passing her back to her daddy. "Bye, baby," I say, waving to her and Rah.

"We'll talk," Rah says to me as I follow Jeremy to the counter and claim our food. I'm so hungry I could eat both orders. I have a lot of thinking to do about my friendships with Rah and Jeremy. Maybe I need to make a list of good and bad qualities for both of them. And whoever has the shorter list of bull wins my time. That'll have to wait until tomorrow. When I get back to Mama's tonight it's going to be late to do anything but get ready for school in the morning. Monday promises to be full, so I'd better enjoy what little time I've got left of my weekend.

~ 8 ~
Culture Shock

"We set da trend so what da fuss and dem all about?"

—BEENIE MAN

The month of February goes by so fast it's a wonder anyone even acknowledges it. I can't believe it's already the first week in March. As usual, Black History Month was barely mentioned at our school, but that won't happen next year. Once the African Student Union is up and running, we'll officially take over the festivities for our month.

The school day went by equally fast and without much excitement, which I'm always thankful for. Mama and I are hard at work helping Netta clean the shop now that all the clients are gone for the day. I brought up the conversation about religion we had in class last week, and Mama and Netta have been on it ever since. And as usual, the conversation is intriguing and just what I need to hear.

"My problem with the way voodoo is portrayed in movies, novels, and other media outlets is not just the ignorant way it's conveyed. The larger problem in my mind is the fact that they separate the religion from its African roots. Usually when you see a conjure woman she looks like Aunt Jemima did before they gave her a perm and put pearls in her ears. She was, and always will be, a mammy figure and I get tired of seeing that shit," Mama says, scrubbing the floor harder with every racist memory she conjures up.

"Lynn Mae, do you remember that time those white women came to us for a divination back in N'awlins?" Netta asks, spraying Windex on all the mirrors before wiping them down with paper towels.

"Yes, I do. They couldn't believe we were priestesses, saying we were too pretty to practice hoodoo the old way. They didn't trust us and walked on down the road to one of the other houses to get a reading, which was just fine with me." Mama puts the mop back in the bucket and wipes the sweat from her brow.

"Me, too. I've never taken too kindly to white folks participating in our religion. They've got their own way and they need to live it," Netta says, and I agree. Mama's ingrained that thought into all of her children's heads. I think Daddy even feels the same way when it comes to his church. I've never seen a white person in his African Methodist Episcopal congregation or any of the similar churches we used to visit when I was younger.

"I agree one hundred percent. That's why when we initiate people now we make them take an oath to never initiate non-Africans into our religion. They can come and witness, but these are our ancestors that we're reclaiming, not theirs." Mama's very clear about that fact.

"That's right, little Jayd," Netta says, continuing with her cleaning. "They've got their own ancestors to worry about paying homage to, and so does every other culture on earth. You don't see us trying to bow down to some other people's gods, do you? That's just plain disrespectful if you ask me, to both our ancestors and theirs." I continue folding the clean towels and listening to the elders in the room. I feel better knowing I'm not alone in my thinking.

"We're the survivors, Jayd, and there's nothing to feel guilty about. Praising our own heritage is just one step in our collective journey to take back what is most important in every human experience: our true selves. It's a sense of empowerment that our ancestors had to shield behind the guise of Catholic saints. But we don't need the veils anymore." Mama puts the mop and bucket in the corner and sits down in one of the empty chairs to let the floor dry. Spring cleaning always takes the best out of us. After I finish putting the fresh towels up I'll move on to organizing the clients' personal hair care boxes.

"We don't have to hide anymore, and I'm so glad for it. I was tired of looking at white faces when praising my African deities," Netta says, recalling worshiping when she was a child. "My nana's still stuck in her old ways to this day, now more out of shame than fear. It's almost as if she's been looking in a European mirror for so long that she can't see an African image staring back at her anymore, no matter how many prayers she can chant in Yoruba." That's some deep shit right there. I feel so blessed to have such strong African women in my lineage. I may have a lot of problems, but loving being black has never been an issue for me.

"It's a shame, Jayd," Mama says. "It's really depressing when I think about it. That's why I practice to myself and try not to worry about what the rest of the world thinks. Whether they consider themselves African or not, I know what I'm doing is for the survivors. I don't have to prove my truth to anyone. I'm too old for that."

"And it's not our job," Netta adds. "The orisha will take care of all of that pettiness. Our job is to take care of them," Netta says, joining Mama on a break. When I finish with the clients' boxes I'll join them before Mama and I walk home. It was such a nice afternoon I decided to park the car at the house and take a stroll for old times' sake.

"When do women get a break? It seems like we're the ones

always taking care of other people," I say, thinking about how Mama holds down the household duties, works with Netta and has her own clientele. I don't mind working hard, but damn, do we ever get to chill for more than a few stolen moments in between chores? Mama and Netta look at each other and laugh at the young woman in the room.

"You'll get a break when you're an ancestor," Netta says, leaning back in her seat. She's looks tired but happy. Netta loves doing hair and working with Mama, and my grandmother feels the same way.

"We have a lot of responsibility on our shoulders, but it's not our job to fight every battle that comes our way. Nor is it our job to go around witnessing to folks," Mama says. "We don't save people, Jayd. People save themselves. And when the orisha call we must answer, not only because it's in our best interest to do so, but also because it's in our blood. Generations depend on us accepting our crowns and all of the hard work that comes with them. You might as well go on and get used to it now, child."

I know Mama's right, but it seems like dudes have an easier life than women do. As Mama says, I can complain all I want, but it'll do me no good. Besides, I know black women set the trends for the world to mimic, so why am I hating on us? No matter how unfair life can get, I know I'm strong enough to take it like the woman I was born to be, crown, mop, and all.

Friday couldn't have come soon enough. This week has been very challenging for me. I've fallen behind on some of my schoolwork, but made up for it by studying during break and lunch. This morning has been filled with the usual quizzes in my first two classes and I'm looking forward to the same in the third.

"Hola, Jayd. Here, I have a note for you," Maggie, my Latina homegirl, says, slipping me the rectangular paper. It's our passing period so we don't have time to catch up, but I do want to know what's been up with my girl. The plans for the Cultural Awareness Festival next week are well underway, with fancy decorations popping up all over campus and getting on my nerves.

"How'd you get this?" I ask, looking down at my name. Who would send me a note through Maggie?

"Emilio sent it to you. He said he wanted to give it to you in class, but he didn't want Jeremy to see. *Ciao bella, mami."* Maggie says, picking up the pace with everyone else around us rushing to third period, including me. I don't want to be late to government. Mrs. Peterson would love to give me my first official tardy of the spring semester and I'm not having that.

"Gracias y hasta luego," I yell after her. I make it to my locker, switch out my books and race to beat the bell. I've successfully avoided talking to Emilio this week, even with him trying to get my attention in the two classes we have together. I can't believe he turned out to be such an ass.

While speed-walking out of the main hall and into the history corridor, I unfold the letter and glance over the beautiful handwriting. Oh my. This boy's really got it bad for me if he's copying orikis for Oshune. The traditional songs praising my mother orisha are always flattering, speaking of her beauty and bountifulness. But this is one of the sexiest orikis I've ever read. At the end of the song are the words *lo siento.* I know he's sorry, but it's too late for that. Whatever small chance Emilio may have had with me is long gone.

"Hey, Jayd. What's got you so dazed?" Jeremy says over my shoulder as he passes me by, beating me to our seats. Jeremy has been my study partner all week long and it's working out well for both of us.

"Oh, nothing," I say, quickly refolding the letter and taking my seat. After Jeremy and I left Simply Wholesome on
Sunday, we talked about everything and cleared the air. Now
things are good between us and I don't want him to have any
reason to cop an attitude again.

"Mrs. Peterson is absent today and I'm going to be your sub,"
an old man says, entering the buzzing classroom. "Please put
your books away. Your teacher has left your quiz and we'll
start in one minute." Jeremy looks at me and makes a funny
face. I'm glad we're back on solid terms. I haven't written his
list down yet, but I know his good points vastly outweigh the
negative. We're from two different cultures with a tangled
past, but who says we can't work it out?

I was grateful for our substitute teacher in third period,
even though he was more boring than watching paint dry.
Mr. Adewale is like a breath of fresh air, even if some of my
classmates stink. Today's topic is interracial dating and has
hit a sore spot with almost everyone in the room. For most of
us, it's a very personal subject and that's why Mr. A's making
us talk about it.

"It's different when black girls date outside of their race
because there aren't enough black men to go around. Y'all,
on the other hand, have it made with all of the available sistahs out there and yet and still y'all date white girls," I say,
staring directly at Del. I saw him kissing a white girl last week
and he knows it, too. I should out his ass right here, but I
know he'd be crucified.

"That's a load of crap and you know it," KJ says. "We don't
have it quite like that because sistahs can throw too much attitude our way, for real."

"Way too much, for real," Money says, throwing his two
cents in the mix and sounding like a parrot.

"So it's okay if you date outside of your race as long as it's because of a personality difference, is that what you're saying?" Mr. Adewale asks, playing devil's advocate even though I know how strongly he feels about this topic. He's disappointed with me dating Jeremy, but Mr. A's the only other dude up here I'm attracted to, and he's too old for me. So what's a girl to do?

"Yeah, it's cool I guess. But some of us just date outside of the race because they like the money on the other side," KJ says, looking dead at me, then Jeremy. He knows he's out of line for that one. Before I can check my ex-fool, Jeremy does the honors.

"And then some see beyond race to how they'll be treated," Jeremy says, taking my hand in his and kissing my knuckles. "I treat my woman like a queen, period."

"Damn, Jayd's got that fool sprung," Shae yells out, making the rest of the class laugh. I'm speechless after Jeremy's confession and apparently so is Mr. Adewale, who's just staring at me as Jeremy and KJ stare at each other. His sandy brown locks look lovely hanging loosely around his shoulders.

"Whatever, man. You and I both know the truth," KJ says, not backing down from his insult.

"You can be of the same race but have very different cultures," I add, hoping that's the end of this conversation. I can tell Jeremy's uncomfortable and so am I. Nigel looks ready to move on, too. He and Jeremy have become good friends and he and Rah are boys for life. The subject is not so easy for him, either.

"I feel you, sister," Seth says, primping his bold side burns in his compact mirror. "That's why I'm starting a club for the gay population at South Bay. We deserve our civil rights, too." I look at Seth in disbelief. Another club? Great, just what we need. How many cliques can one school legally have?

"I'm just saying, why y'all always got to link gay rights with civil rights? They're not the same thing," Nigel says, voicing my sentiments exactly. I'm all for people living how they want to live and it's true, gay people are discriminated against. But linking their struggle for civil liberties is not the same thing my ancestors endured, after toiling for this country without basic human rights for hundreds of years.

"I'd expect you to say something like that," Seth says, rolling his eyes at Nigel, who is about ready to leap out of his chair and sock Seth in his glossy mouth. This is exactly why I didn't want to be in a general education classroom. The environment doesn't lend itself to friendly debate, no matter how diplomatic Mr. A tries to be. It's all or nothing around here. Although I must admit, it is my most entertaining class this semester.

"What the hell is that supposed to mean?" Nigel's temper is on high right about now. Mickey massages her man's hand, but it's not helping to calm him down.

"It means that you're a homophobe. And that's exactly why we need our own club." Matt looks at his friend and shakes his head. Matt's a typical surfer dude, much like Jeremy, but he cares less about academic prowess than Jeremy does. Matt and Seth are the exact opposites yet they're the best of friends.

When I first met them in drama class I thought Matt was Seth's boyfriend, but Matt quickly checked me on that notion. He's been defending his gay homeboy since elementary school and considers him more like a brother than anything else. I know he's got Seth's back, no matter how obnoxious Seth can be.

"I'm not homophobic, dumb-ass. But I am tired of people using the Civil Rights Movement to push their own agenda. You've got your own movements to highlight your cause, don't you?" Nigel looks around the room at KJ and his boys, who nod their heads in agreement. I know most of the black people in here feel the same way and yes, most of the boys are homophobic, unlike Nigel. He doesn't tell most people, but his sister is a lesbian, no matter how much their parents pray for her so-called salvation. Nigel is the first to defend her and will kick anyone's ass who tries to talk shit about her.

"Yes, but the Civil Rights Movement is just that: a movement for civil rights, and gay people are singled out in this country more than anyone else." Seth can't be serious. I want to jump in so bad, but I don't want the spotlight back on me.

"What the hell?" Oops, did I say that out loud?

"Jayd, do you want to add to the debate?" Mr. Adewale asks, putting me on the spot. Why did he do that? Sometimes I think Mr. A loves to challenge me just for fun, but it feels more like torture, even on a good day.

"Oh no, my bad," I say. Nigel looks at me in shock, but he'll just have to ride this one out on his own. The last thing I want to do is make an enemy out of Seth—and, Matt, too, by default. They can make a sistah's life in both drama class and the drama club more difficult than necessary. Even if I am a member of the ASU, drama is still my main love.

Everyone knows that Matt and Seth, as both the main stage producers and prop managers, have Mrs. Sinclair's ear when it comes to auditions and all other important drama business. I don't want to end up like Miss California did when she voiced her personal opinion about gay marriage to one of the judges of Miss USA, who just so happened to be gay. She lost the crown and got clowned on his blog. Knowing Seth, that judge is probably one of his mentors, and I'm not going out like that. We have one more play and a musical before school's out in three months, and I want them to go as smoothly as they can.

"What? Man, please," Nigel says, dismissing Seth's argument—and I have to agree. Seth's taking it a bit too far, although I am all for him starting a club if that's what he really wants to do.

"I'm serious. Whenever I tell someone I'm gay—" Seth begins, but not before Nigel can interject.

"That's what I'm saying. You have to tell someone that you're gay. We don't have to tell anyone we're black." KJ and his crew clap and whistle loudly. I smile and clap my hands under the table.

"It's still the same thing," Seth says, his anger now apparent in his blue eyes. Is he wearing eyeliner?

"No, it isn't. You're still a white boy with all the privileges thereof in this society. Even the gayest white man was still a master back in the day." As the bell rings, ending fourth period, the class is silent while Nigel's words permeate the air like the funky truth that they are. He's right and we all know it. Seth will probably never admit it, but I know he heard Nigel loud and clear.

"Okay, class, that's the bell," Mr. Adewale says, picking up his large textbook and slamming it down on his desk like a gavel. Nigel definitely won that argument and Seth's defeated look says he knows it, too. "Have a good lunch and weekend." We begin to file out of the room and head to lunch. Jeremy and I are going off campus alone. We both need to decompress after that intense discussion.

"Jayd, are you busy tomorrow afternoon? Me and Nellie are going to meet up at my house and discuss the baby shower," Mickey says, rubbing her watermelon-sized belly. She looks cute pregnant, even if she should be picking out her prom dress instead of baby clothes. I know she wants to grill me more about Mrs. Esop possibly coming to the shower, but I don't know if I'm willing to make the personal sacrifice it'll take to get her there.

"Maybe after I get off work," I say, filing out of the class-room with Jeremy right behind me. "We're going to lunch, but I'll hit you up later." Nigel and my girl look at me and Je-remy, who's holding my hand and waiting patiently. Mickey smiles at me and grabs her man's hand as he leads her out of the room. Nigel's always going to want Rah and me back to-gether, no matter how unrealistic it may be.

"Okay, Jayd. Bye, Jeremy," Mickey says, following Nigel to the lunch quad. I already know I'm going to get grilled about this tomorrow. Maybe by then I'll have something really in-teresting to tell her. Not only are we going to lunch, but after I get off work this evening, Jeremy's picking me up from my mom's house in his friend's Benz again and we're going to cruise Sunset Strip in Hollywood all night long. I'm looking forward to having fun with my boy.

"Ready to go, Lady J?" Jeremy asks, claiming my backpack to carry. Mr. Adewale looks at us and shakes his head. I know he doesn't get it, but it's not for him to get. If I want to be with Jeremy that's up to me and Jeremy—no other opinions allowed.

After working all day at the shop I'm tired and funky, but still came to my girl's house to discuss her baby shower. But so far Nellie and Mickey have been doing all the talking. Why am I even here on a Saturday evening, when I could be hang-ing out with Jeremy or by my damn self? I can barely keep my eyes open long enough to pretend like I care about what's going on in Mickey and Nellie's fantasy world. All I can really think about is me and Jeremy.

I didn't get home from our date until almost two this morning. Jeremy and I drove around Hollywood all night long and ended up in Malibu, where we parked and hung out for a while. I forgot how good a kisser he is. I got lost in his touch last night and for the first time in a long time thought about taking the next step with Jeremy. But five minutes in Mickey's world has made me appreciate not making that leap too soon.

Mickey's parents just got home from work and are sitting in front of the television, where they'll most likely remain for the rest of the night. Her father is a garbage man and her mother works at the post office. On Mickey's block her family is the Joneses others aspire to be like. They're what we call hood rich: they have good jobs, everyone's got a ride and they don't seem to want for anything, even with a large family living in a three-bedroom house.

Unlike Mama and Daddy, they extended their home by adding an extra bathroom and a den. Mickey shares a bedroom with her younger sister, and her three brothers have a room across the hall. Their parents have their own bathroom in their room, leaving the hallway bathroom for the children to use.

"Nigel, have you asked your parents if I can move in once the baby's born?" Mickey asks, like they're newlyweds saving for a home. In her mind, maybe that's how her teenage pregnancy appears. But in everyone else's reality it's a very different story.

"Not yet, baby, but I will. You know I want to see both of my babies every day," Nigel says, bending forward and kissing Mickey on the tip of her nose. They look so cute together. I wish I could sit in between my boyfriend's legs on Mama's porch, with her well within viewing range. She'd think I'd lost my mind again. I'm not judging my girl or the way her and her family chill. To each her own, but I know they couldn't be this affectionate in front of Nigel's parents, either.

"When? Nickey Shantae is going to be here in three months,

Nigel." Mickey rubs her stomach for dramatic effect. Nellie rolls her eyes at our girl and tosses the baby catalogue she's viewing onto the pile of others on the porch. She replaces it with a baby name book, which is unnecessary. Mickey's had her daughter's name picked out since she knew what a daughter was. I doubt any name in that book will sway her decision.

"Can we consider a different name? How about Madison?" Nellie says. Mickey laughs at our girl's suggestion but Nellie's serious.

"I like her name," I say. I know my goddaughter's listening and I want her to feel my love. "At least it's original and created out of love."

"Exactly, just like my name. My daddy bought my mom a Mickey Mouse doll on their first date. She liked it so much that he bought her something with Mickey Mouse on it every time he gave her a gift from then on," Mickey says, beaming like the spoiled daughter she is. I never knew there was so much sentiment behind her name.

I can hear a song come on the television inside, and start moving my shoulders to the beat. I'm not sure which band it is, but I know I've heard Jeremy playing this song before, and I love it.

"What's the name of that song playing on the commercial?" I ask my friends, hoping that maybe one of them will recognize it. I know Chance and Nellie listen to alternative music on occasion.

"Okay, Ms. ASU. You can't be black and love white music. It just ain't natural," Mickey says. Both Nellie and I look at our girl, neither surprised by what can fly out of her fuchsia colored lips at any moment. But I am shocked sometimes at the way she thinks about the world.

I look at Mickey and realize that even though we're both

black and from the same hood, we live in two different cultures. She and her family don't ever want to leave Compton; they're content not travelling, reading, or even considering living anywhere else but here. Mickey thinks living in Compton is the most real shit ever. Even if she would prefer to live in LA with Nigel and his family, she'd love it if he'd move back to her neck of the woods.

"You know rock music is black music, too." I'm glad Nigel's got some sense. Maybe it'll rub off on her and my goddaughter, too.

"Whatever. I think you all think too much about being black and white. We're all one, just like the motto for the Cultural Festival says. Why can't we all just get along?" Nellie asks with her silly self.

"Because, Rodney King, it ain't that simple. We're not making fondue in this country. No one's going to melt down my culture." I need to get out of here before I really go off. I wish I could talk to Mr. Adewale on the phone sometimes, especially when I feel my head getting hot like it is now.

"Making fon-what?" Mickey asks, her button nose all scrunched up like she got a whiff of the fresh dog shit the loose pit bull across the street just laid. He's running around the yard almost choking himself with the tight leather strap hanging around his neck. What good is a leash if no one's holding the other end? You'd never see anything like this in Redondo Beach.

"Fondue," Nellie answers like she's an authority on the subject. "It's melted cheese. You usually dip bread in it. But Chance and I went to a restaurant that melted chocolate, too." Mickey looks completely unimpressed by Nellie's knowledge of the fancy feast.

"Around here we call that a grilled cheese sandwich. Which reminds me, it's time for me and baby to eat," Mickey says, making her way up off the porch. It is getting late and I know Mama will start to worry if I'm not on my way to Inglewood soon. And all of this food talk has got my stomach growling, too.

"And on that note, I think I'll check out." I rise from my comfy spot on the dilapidated brick porch with my keys in hand. It was nice chilling with my crew, but it's definitely time to go. Besides, Rah couldn't be here and has been blowing my cell up all evening. I suppose I should call him back, but for what? I'd rather walk across hot coals than talk anymore about Rah's drama in the house of hell he's created with Sandy.

"Okay, Jayd. And I'm looking forward to positive results with that situation you're responsible for," Mickey says, like we're secret agents on a mission to get her baby-daddy's mama to like her. I'd hate to be around when Mrs. Esop pops her delusional bubble. Mickey's my girl and I'm going to try my best to make her happy—but not by sacrificing myself in the process.

"I'm all over it, Mickey. Bye, y'all," I say to Nellie and Nigel before heading to my car parked on the street. It's almost a half hour from here to my mom's apartment, and I need to stop somewhere in between for dinner. I have a full day of heads to braid tomorrow and I have to study in the afternoon. With the rest of my busy weekend, I'm looking forward to getting some good sleep tonight.

"Bye, Jayd. And my boy said to holla when you get a min," Nigel says, winking at me from across the porch. I get in my ride and slam the door at the thought of talking to Rah.

Rah's not slick, monitoring my movements through Nigel. I haven't spoken to Rah since I saw him at Simply Wholesome last weekend. I'm not sure I know what to say.

If I tell him I'm thinking of getting back with Jeremy, he wouldn't take me seriously anyway. Maybe Mickey has a point about black and white mixing: it's just not natural. But if that's true, then why does being with Jeremy feel like home?

~ 9 ~
I'm Not

*"I've got to let you know/
You're one of my kind."*

—INXS

*"**O**h, sweetie, you know I would be with you if I could, but it's just not the right time," Maman's lover says to her with tears streaming down his face. Maman looks into his blue eyes, searching for the truth with her mystical green eyes, also moist from crying. They appear to be outside at night in the rain. They both look around nervously, in fear of being caught by each other's spouses or people who don't like interracial dating, yet they stay where they are.*

"Do you love me?" Maman's words ring through the air like a bell. Love. How can a white man living in the Jim Crow South truly love a black woman? And how could she want his love?

"Marie, how can you ask me that? After everything we've been through, after all the sacrifices I've made so that we can be together, you would doubt my feelings for you? Yes, of course I love you," her lover says, kissing her on the top of her head. They're soaked from standing out in the rain for so long. They didn't have umbrellas back in Maman's time, or what?

"Then let's go, now. Let's run away together," Maman says, sounding excited like a hopeful schoolgirl. "Take me away

now, before Jon Paul finds out about our affair and kills us both." Maman breaks down in her lover's arms, trembling from cold and fear. "Don't leave me here with him any longer, please. If you love me take me away from this evil place. New Orleans is not good for us, my love." Maman's lover looks down into her eyes, almost giving in to her powerful gaze, but he turns away just in time. I guess he knows all about Maman's gift.

"Marie, when the time is right you know we'll leave. But now is not the time," he says, his tears again welling up. This dude's really feeling Maman, but he's not strong enough to do what it takes to be with her. Even white boys get lynched under Jim Crow if they choose to hang with black folks—literally.

"Why not? Why can't we just run away up North, or do like your friends who moved to California and got married? Yes, we can be free to be open with our love there." Maman's lover lifts her face from his chest and looks at her solemnly.

"I have to get married," he says to her as if he's just been issued a death sentence. "You know I wouldn't if it weren't for my family inheritance, Marie, but I can't afford to lose my share." Maman's hopeful look hardens as she pushes away from their embrace. This must be before either of them had children. Maman looks younger than I've ever seen her in any of my other visions.

"That's what it's always been about, hasn't it?" Maman says in a cryptic voice, reminding me more of our evil next-door neighbor, Esmeralda, than herself. Her tears become waves of passionate cries as her emotion overwhelms her. I wish I could hug her, but in this dream I'm just a quiet observer. "Enjoy your money and your white woman. You can both go straight to hell!" Maman takes off down the dark street, water splashing underneath her sandals as she runs away, never looking back.

"Marie, wait!" her lover yells after her, but it's too late.
Maman is long gone.

"Jayd, can a brotha get a ride to work this morning, or
what?" Bryan asks, interrupting my final few moments of
sleep. If the alarm hasn't gone off then I know it's too early
for me to be having this conversation.

"Waking me up is not the way to get what you want,
Bryan," I say, turning over in my bed and pinning my pillow
over my face. Maybe he'll go away if I ignore him.

"Consider me your personal alarm clock," he says. Bryan's
such an ass. "And you need to hook my braids up, too."

"Don't push it," I say, flipping the blankets back to start
my day. What a strange dream. I never knew that Maman
wanted to run off with her white boy. From all of the other visions I've had, it was always her lover who wanted to be with
her. That sure does put things into perspective a bit with Jeremy and me. I want to be with him and he wants to be with
me. Unlike in Maman's day, we can be together, so why
shouldn't we?

I'll give it some more thought as the day progresses, but
the more I think about it the fewer problems I see with me
and Jeremy giving our relationship another shot. So what if
everyone hates on us and talks shit about the black girl from
the hood and her rich, white surfer dude. That's what they
already do. Besides, I'm not here to please anyone else. My
happiness is what matters, and so far Jeremy makes me very
happy.

When I arrived at school this morning Jeremy was nowhere to be found. I guess he decided to take the day off and
I can't blame him. If I could have slept in I would've done
the same thing. But Mama doesn't believe in letting me stay
home if there's nothing wrong, no matter how sleep de-

prived a sistah might be. He also hasn't texted me back this morning, so I know he's either knocked out or surfing. It must be nice to have such a chill existence, which is opposite of everything I know.

It's been a busy Monday morning, collecting all of my weekly assignments and getting last week's work back. I did well on my quizzes, but my homework grades could be better. I'm not comfortable slipping down a single point in my class average, and at the rate I'm going, my A average will be an A-minus on the mid-semester progress reports if I don't up my game soon in all of my classes.

After speech and debate class, Mr. Adewale called an ASU meeting for those of us still interested in the club. There are still a few technicalities to work out with the administration on the club's official formation, but Mr. Adewale and Ms. Toni are hopeful that it'll all work out in time for Cultural Awareness Day. With the festival next week, we need to decide on the club's participation categories and what kind of food we're going to sell at our booth, just in case we are able to participate in the day-long festivities.

"Okay, so we've got to decide on a theme, which will include a presentation or a performance, customary attire, music, and of course, food." Mr. Adewale likes the sound of that, I see. I'll have to bring him a plate from Mama if he likes to eat that much. "Any suggestions?" he asks, filling out the official club entry form on his clipboard while we all eat our lunches. The usual crew is here, including Misty, KJ, and followers. But unlike last time, Emilio's not here and I'm not surprised. I never responded to the letter he sent me through Maggie and he's avoided me today. I don't mean to be rude, but he needs to back off and I'm glad he's finally getting the message.

"Yeah, I say we go in chains with that fool holding the whip,"

KJ says, pointing at Chance. Every time I think he can't get any more ignorant, KJ goes and proves me wrong. How could he have ever reminded me of Rah?

"I think you should grow the hell up," Nellie says, defending her man. I know it's a major sacrifice of her primping time to come to our meeting, but she belongs here just as much as the rest of us, including KJ's dumb ass. I think Chance convinced her to come, even if I did ask her several times to offer the club her support. How come boys can get girls to do things when their homegirls can't?

"We weren't just slaves, KJ," Mr. Adewale says, putting him in his place. It's about time someone did. KJ gets away with clowning around in most of his other classes because he's a star athlete. But Mr. Adewale couldn't care less about KJ's scoring average.

"I think we should perform a scene from *Fences,*" Chance offers, smiling at me. He's performing a small role in the drama club's performance at the Cultural Awareness assembly and still has my back for my play suggestion. What a sweet friend. I don't know what I'd do without him in my life. He may be Nellie's boyfriend, but Chance will always be my leading man when it comes to the stage.

"Man, we ain't performing no punk ass, lame ass, stupid ass play," KJ says, making his crew laugh. Why are they even here? I know they don't care about African American and diaspora issues. All they really want is to say that they're down with the black club on campus. When it's time to do the work they'll be nowhere to be found.

"I think it's a great idea," Mr. Adewale says, glancing at Chance and then at KJ, pissed at the irony of the situation. It's our first ASU event and a white boy is the one making the most relevant suggestions. "Nigel, would you be interested in performing a scene from the play?" Nigel looks at Mr. Adewale like he's crazy. I'm not surprised by my boy's reaction, but I am a little disappointed.

"I think it's a good idea, but I'm not the one for this role," Nigel says, leaning back in his seat and watching Mickey look at herself in the mirror. Nellie's doing the same thing. I hope some of Mr. A's consciousness rubs off on all of us, because we're in desperate need of some righteous guidance.

"I can do it," Chance says, shocking everyone except for me. I know he's a good actor and can play the hell out of the lead character's part. Chance and I used to rehearse scenes from the play last year, just for the hell of it. When we first read it together we loved it and had fun developing the characters. "And Jayd can play Ruth. She knows that part like the back of her hand."

"Okay, then it's settled. We'll offer a scene from August Wilson's play for the opening assembly," he says, writing it down in ink before anyone can protest. "We only have about a minute left to discuss the festival. So, what's on the menu?" Mr. Adewale tries to move on, but KJ's not having it.

"Hold up a minute," KJ says, leaning forward in his seat and shaking his nasty-ass toothpick in the air. He just finished a burrito, and part of it is on the tiny wooden stick. "How's a white boy going to play a black man?" KJ asks, now standing he's so pissed. He should've thought of that before he dismissed the idea so quickly.

"I guess we'll find that out at the assembly. Jayd and Chance, I'm counting on you to rehearse on your own. We look forward to seeing the scene at the next meeting. As for the menu and theme, we'll take a silent vote after class tomorrow," Mr. Adewale says, adjourning the meeting as the bell rings so we can all get to our fifth period classes.

"This is some foul shit, man," Del says, getting up with the rest of us. He looks at Chance like he wants to beat his ass, but Del's too chicken for a move like that. And as thin as Chance is, he can still defend himself when necessary, with or without his boys behind him.

"You should've thought of that before y'all were too proud to perform," I say. "Maybe next time you'll step up like real black men instead of the little boys y'all are acting like now." I grab my backpack off the floor, ready to get to drama class.

"Shut the hell up, white-boy lover," KJ says. Misty smiles at her man's ignorance. Chance looks like he's about to spit on KJ, and he should. If he only knew the truth about his heritage, Chance wouldn't have to put up with so much hating from these suckers at South Bay. But as long as I'm dating a white boy, I will have to put up with these idiots.

"And I fell for a white boy after being your girlfriend, KJ," I say, stepping up to him and looking him dead in the eye. "So what kind of man does that make you?" Misty steps in front of her man and in my face, ready to throw down over his stupid ass, as usual. I thought she learned her lesson after I stripped her of her dreams, but I guess not.

"A damned lucky one," she says, her hands firmly set on her wide hips, like she's going to do something. I wish the trick would. She knows I'm not the one to play with and KJ's ass has never been worth fighting over.

"Okay, let's all calm down," Mr. Adewale says, breaking us up before it gets too ugly. None of us notice the visitor in the room.

"Well, what do we have here?" Mrs. Bennett asks, entering at the tail end of our meeting, unannounced and uninvited. Misty backs up and smiles at me like I just walked into her trap. What the hell is she up to now?

"Can I help you?" Mr. Adewale asks, looking at the clock above our heads. We have three minutes until the tardy bell rings, but I'm not going anywhere until I know why she's here.

"Well, actually I think I can be of help to you," she says, handing Mr. Adewale a slip. "I heard your little club was in need of an adviser so I volunteered, since I am responsible for you while you're on probation, Mr. Adewale," she says, slyly. "I also don't think a junior faculty member should hold club meetings in their room." Mrs. Bennett looks at me and Misty, her cold blue eyes shimmering. Misty takes a step back and nods her head, but in recognition of what?

"With all due respect, Mrs. Bennett, I can host whatever groups I want to in my classroom." Mr. Adewale carefully reads the paper in front of him and his face gets more red with each word his eyes absorb.

"But I'm your mentor teacher," she says, pointing to the paper. "And I think this group needs proper supervision. And what's wrong with holding the meetings in my room?" Mrs. Bennett suggests. The bell's about to ring and the other students begin to head slowly toward the door. Nobody wants to miss how this showdown is going to end.

"What's wrong with it is that we are fine where we are." The two teachers lock bright eyes and I'm loving the action. It's about time someone other than Ms. Toni stood up to this broad. "And I've already pulled in Ms. Toni as the supervising adviser, no offense."

"I'm well aware of your request, but she's so busy with ASB that the administration is concerned about her taking on too much. I, on the other hand, only chair the Advanced Placement group, and after the exams in May I'll be as free as a bird." Mrs. Bennett's not slick. She's going to destroy our club without a second thought if she gets the chance, and we can't let that happen.

"We'll see about that," Mr. Adewale says, glaring at Mrs. Bennett, who turns around and walks out of the room.

Everyone follows suit and heads to fifth period, with less than a minute to get there. I'm not worried about receiving a tardy in drama, especially because no one's paying attention to me too much since I'm not performing in this play.

"Mr. Adewale, can I do anything to help?" I ask, walking up to him on my way out. The rest of my crew is already gone, so it's just me and him.

"They're trying to stop the club from officially forming before the festival, if at all," Mr. Adewale says, frustrated. I look past him at Laura and Reid talking with Mrs. Bennett outside. I know they had something to do with this. And I also know Misty's not in the clear. She's been their mole, sneaking information from our meetings back to them. And like any other pest, she needs to be evacuated from our space. Like Mama's enemies, mine haven't learned that I'm not the one to mess with, but they will, soon enough.

"Just tell me what to do and I'll do it," I say. I wish I could cheer him up. "Mrs. Bennett isn't that bad. Her bark is worse than her bite," I lie. We both know Mrs. Bennett's the one broad up here who can get in our way.

"We can pray for justice and work toward it," he says, reminding me of his lineage's gift. Mr. Adewale fights for justice and I know he's going to have his ancestors all over this one. I'll worry about fighting Misty and her evil ways and leave the rest to the warriors in Mr. A's lineage. It's about time he showed us what he can do.

Trying to get the club in order before next week's celebration has proven to be no easy task. Monday's bombshell from Mrs. Bennett put it all into perspective for us: if we're serious about the African Student Union being a viable, productive group we have to get our personal issues in check, and I think we've done well. Misty has been rather quiet since the meeting, but she's not fooling me. I know she's trying to sabotage the group and I will prove it one way or another.

Friday came so quickly I didn't even realize the week had come and gone. We have to wait until next week to find out if our club proposal was accepted. Until then we're going to walk as if it has been, per Mr. Adewale's example. He's convinced that justice will prevail, with Ms. Toni as our senior club adviser—not Mrs. Bennett's conniving self, no matter how bad she thinks she is. And by the way he's wearing his confident crown, I have nothing but faith in Mr. A.

When we decided to meet over at Nigel's house for tonight's session I thought we'd be in for the night which is our usual mode of operation. The guys smoke, the girls listen to music while a good movie plays on the wide screen. But apparently our crew has other plans. After school, I worked at Netta's until closing, where I also touched up my Uncle Bryan's braids. Rah also came in and got his head washed and braided, not saying a word about seeing me and Jeremy together last weekend. It was nice to get back in Rah's head. No matter what type of relationship he may have with Trish and Sandy, I know I'll always be his stylist and I'm always thankful for the dough.

"So where are we going?" Mickey asks, waddling to Nigel's king-sized bed and lying down. Nigel's so lucky to have a room as nice and spacious as this. Nigel and Rah are putting on their Timberland boots, ready to work. They look so cute in their matching mechanic jumpsuits and white T-shirts, but I'd never tell them that. Mickey yawns loudly as she stretches out like a cat across the foot of the king-size bed. She looks exhausted. "I can't move too fast these days." She's right about that. It took her damn-near five minutes to make it up the flight of stairs that lead to Nigel's room. That baby's finally slowing our girl down.

"We have to go work in the pit for Trish's brother, at this race in your neck of the woods," Rah says to Chance, making light of the fact that he's going to kick it with Trish and her kin again. We haven't hashed out all of our issues, but decided to make peace with each other for the time being. However, I'm still not cool chilling with either one of his exes.

"Ask me if I give a damn," I say, sucking on the sour lemon in my iced tea. Nellie and Chance look at me, Nellie rolling her eyes at my response. I'm too tired to be tactful.

"We're all going together. Come on, it'll be fun," Rah says, walking over to me and rubbing my bare arms with the back of his hands. The subtle scent from his Egyptian musk lotion rubs off on my arms slightly. I hope I don't end up mad at him by the end of the night because every time I catch a whiff of my arm he'll be on my mind, smelling good.

"Okay, let's get going. I don't want to miss a thing," Nellie says, more excited than I thought she'd be about going to a street race. I drove Chance's car and felt the rush. But I'm not sure about going to an actual race on a Friday night. Not only is it dangerous, but we could also get into some real trouble should the police decide to raid the spot. Mama would kill me if I ended up in jail or dead.

"Will I have somewhere to sit down?" Mickey asks, making her way up off the bed. "I wouldn't mind watching those white boys drive. They always have nice whips." I feel my girl on that one. After driving the flyy-ass Benz Jeremy's friend let him roll last weekend I can see why they do what they do. But I'm still not the one to get caught up drag racing. I respect Nigel's and Rah's ability to hustle on the side, but just once I wish they'd pick something that involved a little less risk on their behalf.

"Yeah, baby. You can sit in the stands with everyone else while we work," Nigel says, opening the bedroom door and leading the way out. We head out, ready for tonight's festivities, even if I'm not so sure about this one.

"Coming?" Rah asks, offering me his hand. I reluctantly take it and rise from my post on the futon. Rah smiles at me as I walk out. He knows I like fast cars as much as anyone. The first time I drove Rah's Legend I was sprung on speed. And driving my friends' cars hasn't helped my looming addiction.

When we make it down the stairs and into the foyer, ready to leave, Mrs. Esop comes through the front door from what looks like an expensive shopping trip.

"Good evening," Mrs. Esop says, greeting us all as she walks inside.

"Hi, Mom," Nigel says as the rest of us say our hellos in unison. Nigel and Rah instinctively help her with her bags. Mickey, Nellie, and I watch in awe as the boys put the Prada, Louis Vuitton and Gucci bags down in the living room before rejoining us by the front door. Chance doesn't bat an eye: I guess he's used to the name-brand regulars in his household.

"What a busy day," Mrs. Esop says, removing her hat and fanning herself with it. "Shopping always takes the breath out of me. But I must look fabulous for the sorority picnic tomorrow," she says, winking at me. I don't know how to tell her, but I can't see myself ever fitting into her world.

"I know what you mean, Mrs. Esop. The mall takes a lot out of me, too," Mickey says, trying to make small talk. Mrs. Esop sneers at Mickey, interrupting her.

"My dear, I don't shop at malls," Mrs. Esop says with her nose as high up in the air as it can possibly get. Mickey lowers her head in shame as Mrs. Esop walks past her without batting an eye. What a cold broad.

"Mom, you're going to have to show Mickey some respect,

especially once she and the baby move in," Nigel says, trying
to land the bomb and run—but not a chance his mom is
going to let that one sit. Mrs. Esop stops in her Prada tracks
before she reaches the living room and looks at her son like
he's a stranger. As she places both hands on her hips, we all
stay put. I knew there was a hood girl behind her expensive,
holier-than-thou demeanor.

"Tell me my son was the only person you were sleeping
with when you found out you were pregnant," Mrs. Esop
says directly to an already shook-up Mickey. The accusation
catches my girl off guard and she doesn't know how to respond. "In all honesty, Mickey, you should've had an abortion if you didn't know who the father was. And son, what
the hell is wrong with you? Where do you think you live,
Nigel? In the projects somewhere? We don't allow baby-mamas
or their little bastards to live in our home," she says, cutting
her teeth and lowering her tone. I think it's safe to say Mrs. Esop
won't be attending the shower after all.

"Hey, I've got my baby-mama living with me, and we don't
live in the projects—and my daughter's no one's bastard,"
Rah says, standing up to Mrs. Esop. But his situation is not a
very helpful example.

"Yes, Rah, and that is unfortunate," Mrs. Esop says, soften-
ing her look and tone, but not by much. "Your parents are
not here to guide you properly, and that's different. And I'm
also convinced that the child Mickey's carrying belongs to
someone else, unlike your daughter." Rah backs off, satisfied
with her justification for the time being. Besides, this really
isn't our fight so we shouldn't get too involved.

"Mama, how many times do I have to tell you this is my
baby?" Nigel says, holding a teary-eyed Mickey by her wide
waist. I feel for my girl, but they did put this on themselves. I
can't really blame Mrs. Esop for reacting. She's protecting

her baby just like Nigel's protecting his, even if I don't agree with how either one of them is going about it.

"I don't care how many times you say those words to me, Nigel Esop. I'll never, ever believe that the baby in that girl's stomach belongs to you," she says, barely acknowledging Mickey's presence or her feelings. "We can't force her to have a paternity test before the baby is born, but we can sure as hell insist on it as soon as that child comes out," she says, pointing at Mickey. "But I don't need a blood test to prove a damn thing. I know you're not the father and I also know you're not stupid," she says, still pointing her perfectly manicured finger at Mickey and Nigel, who both feel the wrath of her words. "Enjoy the good life now, little missy, because your fantasy is going to end when that baby of yours is born."

"Mom, that's enough," Nigel says, holding a now sobbing Mickey in his arms. I've never seen my girl this upset before. Mrs. Esop collects herself, checks her hair in the large foyer mirror where we can all see our reflections, and walks into the living room without another word. She's a cold bitch, no doubt.

"Let's get going before we're late," Nellie says, setting us back on our mission. We move out the front door, but all of us are still stuck in Mrs. Esop's tongue lashing. Mickey looks completely humiliated, and I'm positive that was Mrs. Esop's intention.

"Can you really blame her?" my mom says in my head. *"If Nigel were my son, I'd be suspicious of some fast girl trying to latch on to him, too."*

"Mom, that's not what happened," I think back. I get into my car and my friends get into theirs. Since Rah's going to be working tonight, I'm driving him around for a change. Besides, it'll be good for Trish to see that we're still hanging tight while she's only hanging on by a thin thread.

"Girl, please. Mickey found herself a winner in Nigel. She'd

better hope that baby is his, or else his mama's going to have her ass in a sling. Later," she says, leaving me to focus on the road ahead.

"That was brutal back there," Rah says, breaking the silence as we head toward Redondo Beach. I don't know if he could tell my mom just dropped in for a psychic visit, but I was thinking the same thing.

"Yeah, she didn't have to call Mickey out like that. She's a woman, too."

"Not like Mickey she's not, or at least not anymore." We all know the story of how Mr. and Mrs. Esop wanted to move their children out of Compton to a more upwardly mobile community. "And no matter what happens, Mrs. Esop will always remind Mickey that she's not the kind of woman she wants her son to marry. Mark my words, whether or not the baby belongs to Nigel, she'll never let Mickey have their last name."

Poor Mickey. I'm not one to give up on something I really want, but if fighting a losing battle, I say retreat while you still can. Mickey needs to consider all of her options instead of depending solely on Nigel making it work out with his parents. This is quite a mess she's created and she's got to be the one to clean it up.

~ 10 ~
A Hot Mess

"They don't want to see us unite/
All they want us to do is keep on fussing and fighting."

—BOB MARLEY

When we get to the empty football field, the stands are packed. The cars are parked on the field, each fabulous in its own way. We park in the lot above the field and walk down. Mickey's still visibly upset about her lashing, but the excitement in the air is getting to her, too.

"We've got to get to the pit. The race is about to start," Rah says, walking off toward the other side of the field with Nigel right behind him. Nigel looks like he doesn't want to leave Mickey alone. I walk over and take my girl by the arm, letting them both know I've got her.

"I've got this. Go handle your business," I say as Nigel follows Rah down the the bleachers. Mickey slowly follows Nellie toward a seat. The bleachers are packed, and there are a few faces here from school, but the majority are folks I don't recognize. Watching our boys run down the bleachers, I notice Jeremy and his beach crew on the field. What are they doing here?

"Hey, I'm going down to the field," Chance says as Nellie and Mickey take a seat.

"I'm going, too," I say, making sure my girl is settled before I go check the scene out. I want to see all the fast cars up close and personal. I also want to check out Jeremy without tipping Rah off. The last thing I need is to hear his mouth about some shit.

"Y'all can't just leave us here," Nellie says. "Come on, Mickey, we can sit farther down." Mickey looks like she wants to cuss Nellie out for making her move, but instead she gets up and follows us.

When we make it down to the field, Jeremy and his boys are admiring their fancy rides. Jeremy walks over to me and gives me a hug, glad to see me at their illegal gathering.

"A 1969 Camaro Yenko Clone 427, red leather interior to match the paint job. Sweet," Chance says, and by the mesmerized look on Jeremy's face, he's just as excited about the new addition as his boy is. Nellie looks anything but impressed with the old car. Mickey sits down on the last row of bleachers and makes herself comfortable.

"Man, I was going to get one of these, but the truck was a necessary evil," Jeremy's older brother Justin says, walking around their eldest brother Mike's latest acquisition like a wolf eyeing its prey. All the dudes are salivating over the hot ride. I'm not a hater like Nellie, but I don't get the love affair between men and cars.

"Check that one out. A 1968 SS 396," Jeremy says, eyeing another classic arrival. "I want to take that car on the bend, but I guess I'll settle for racing this piece of shit," Jeremy says, pointing to his own car.

"You're not seriously going to race, are you?" I ask. Jeremy and Chance look down at me and smile. I guess I'm the baby of the crew, in more ways than one. How come I didn't know about this side of our boys?

"Time to burn out, dude," Terry, one of Jeremy's beach friends says. I watch as everyone lines up behind the sidelines, ready to witness the race. Trish's brother parks his tricked out Mazda in line with the other cars, ready to win. I must admit, Rah and Nigel worked their asses off on that car. I can't wait to see them all in action.

"This is the best birthday ever," Maxi, one of the freshman ASB members says, walking toward the starting line where the five hotrods line up, including Jeremy's classic Mustang and Chance's Nova. Nellie and I take our seats next to Mickey, who's eating a bag of pretzels. Nellie takes a compact mirror out of her purse and eyes her perfect curls, as if that's the most important thing going on around her.

"Nellie, how can you concentrate on your hair when your man is about to street race—illegally, might I add?" Usually Nellie's the prude, but ever since she and Chance consummated their relationship, my girl's become a bit more laid back and stuck up at the same time, if that's even possible.

"Relax, Jayd. It's all business," she says, not taking her eyes off her hair. "Do you know how much money they get if they win?"

"Money? So they're gambling, too? We're all going to jail." I throw my hands up in the air for dramatic effect but she's not feeling me. "I just wanted to watch a movie, maybe hang out a little bit," I say, voicing my view of how I thought the evening would turn out. If Mama knew I was here she'd shit a brick and then throw it at me.

"We are hanging out and you can pretend you're watching a movie. Here, stand next to me," she says, rising from her seat and hanging over the rail separating the stands from the field.

"Drivers, show me your stuff," Maxi says, waving the two yellow flags in the air while all the drivers rev their engines. The tires spin, burning tracks into the virgin dirt and officially starting the race. "Staging set," she yells out. The cars get into a straight line, the drivers all focused on the finish line up ahead. I look around, paranoid that any minute the cops are going to show up and haul all our asses away. No one else seems worried about getting caught. If we were in Compton we'd be in booking by now.

"This is my favorite part," Nellie says. I see she's become quite the groupie. It's one thing to drive fast for fun and another to do it for money. "One day I'm going to get my chance to wave the flag." Being the pretty girl who starts the race is another type of crown for Nellie. No wonder she's suddenly so interested in drag racing.

The cars stop spinning their tires and get ready to race. Jeremy looks up at me from his ride and winks, sending a flush of energy up from the middle of my stomach through the front of my shirt. Something about seeing Jeremy behind the wheel under these circumstances is more exciting than usual. I hope Rah didn't see that from where he and Nigel are posted on the other side of the field in the makeshift pit. Maxi quickly brings the flags down to her side and the cars take off on both sides of her. I wonder if other girls in her position ever get hit.

"Doesn't that look fun?" Nellie asks, her eyes glued to the fast scene. Maxi turns around, jumping up and down and screaming for her man to win the first round. After the first lap, we all get into the race. Jeremy and Chance are holding their own, but this race is between the Mazda and the Mustang. All the other cars are just filling.

"It's the last lap. Come on, Chance," Nellie says, rooting for her man. But it's no use. Trish's brother's got this race in the bag.

"The Mazda wins!" Maxi yells, hyping the crowd even more. Nigel and Rah give each other dap for their good work and I'm proud of my boys. When it comes to cars, basketball, and music, Rah knows what he's doing. I wish the same were true when it comes to us.

Me and my girls head down to the field to greet our boys, even if two of them did lose.

"Chance, why do you drive that old thing?" Nellie's never been any good at showing empathy. Chance just lost the race and the money, but she couldn't care less about that. All Nellie's really worried about is her image. Rah waves at me from his and Nigel's post next to Trish's brother. I guess Trish didn't come after all. Noticing us across the field, Trish's brother, Lance, looks in our direction and smiles at Nellie, who smiles back. I don't like the look in either of their eyes.

"Okay, I'm out. I have a long day tomorrow and it starts early," I say, leaving them to their mess. I have to be in Compton by seven in the morning, which means if I get home in the next thirty minutes I can manage a good six hours of sleep.

"It's the weekend. Where are you going in such a rush?" Jeremy asks, getting out of his ride and walking over to me, looking disappointed. I'm not happy about it either, but work is work and when it comes to my lineage, there are never any excuses.

"I have to work, but you looked good out there, Mr. Weiner," I say, trying to avoid his kiss—but I can't. Jeremy kisses me soft and slow, just how I like it. If it keeps feeling this good we might get ourselves into some serious trouble before it's all said and done.

"I'll call you tomorrow. Be safe," Jeremy says, letting me go and walking back to his car. I was hoping Rah didn't see that, but from the smoke I can almost see coming out of his ears, I'd say he saw it all. I'll deal with his jealousy issues tomorrow. Right now I have to get home and rest up for a busy workday tomorrow. I wave to the rest of my friends and head back up the bleachers and away from the field. I have money of my own to get, and it starts with proper sleep.

This weekend proved to be one of our busiest weekends to date. It got a little tense for a moment when the clients had to wait longer than usual to get their heads done by Netta, but with a touch of Mama's lavender spray everything was calm for the rest of the weekend. Last night I went straight to bed without answering Rah's calls or Jeremy's texts. They both know the deal once I get on my hustle. And today was just as busy, leaving me no time to myself this weekend.

I did talk to Jeremy briefly. He was excited about surfing his Sunday away. Rah's pissed about seeing Jeremy and me kiss, but what can I say? Now he knows how I feel every time Trish touches him. Jealousy is a bitch, or two in Rah's case, and I'm tired of dealing with both of them, especially when I can put all that energy toward a healthy relationship with Jeremy.

By the time I get back to Mama's this evening, Mama and Daddy are at it again. I could hear them shouting on my way down the block and it's only gotten louder since I walked in the front door. I was looking forward to a quiet night of studying, but I can see that wish has gone to hell.

"Another heffa or the same one?" Mama asks, holding a sock in her hand and shaking it in Daddy's face. Daddy towers over her five-foot-eight frame, but looks like a little boy in her presence once Mama gets hot. "Answer me! It's important, and don't you dare lie to me," Mama says, vigorously shaking the balled-up clothing at my grandfather. Jay and Bryan are watching the scene from their bedroom. We all feel helpless to stop it.

"Hey," I say, quickly passing them by in the dining room. Before I make it to Mama's room, Mama speaks to me.

"Jayd, as soon as you put your things down, go in the spirit room and get to work. Your assignment's on the kitchen table. I'll be there in a second," she says. I can feel her eyes intently focused on her husband, even with my back to her. Mama must've found out about Daddy's visitor last weekend. I'd hate to be him right now.

"What difference does it make, Lynn Mae? All you know is that a church member came by to see me. You don't know anything else." Daddy knows he's lying through his teeth. Mama knows everything. She just wants the confession for ammunition.

"Church lady? Church ladies make juju bags, too, fool. This little gift of yours was given to you by someone, and if it was that same heffa who brought you that stiff-ass cake a few months ago, you need to tell me."

"Tell you for what? So she can come up missing?" Daddy asks. I can see the fear in his face as he waits for Mama's response. You shouldn't ask a question you don't want to know the answer to.

"I don't work like that and you know it," Mama says between her teeth. She's so pissed I can feel her heart pounding as I walk past her and into the kitchen. I want to get out of harm's way as soon as possible, because this feels like one of those throwing-objects kind of fights. And I don't want to be anywhere near the two of them when shit starts flying.

"Yes, Lynn Mae. It's the same woman," I hear Daddy admit, defeated yet again by Mama's will. "Are you happy now?" Daddy asks, sitting down in one of the four dining chairs around the table.

"Happy?" Mama asks, her voice quivering. "Who the hell would be happy living like this?" I look back at Mama before I step out of the kitchen door. If she's not happy, then why does she put up with this shit? Mama's such a powerful woman, with her own money in the bank. If I were her I would've been gone a long time ago. I know she says it's because no one's driving her out of her own home, but it has to be more than that. What sensible person would want to stay in a burning house?

"Don't get it twisted, Jayd. Mama loves that man. She'll go to bat for him any day," my mom says, answering my

thought as I walk through the backyard and into the spirit room. *"I remember when Daddy had a heart attack when I was in high school. I thought Mama was going to die, her nerves were on edge so bad. Netta stepped in and took care of the household while Mama sat by Daddy's bedside day and night until he made a full recovery. You know she petitioned the orisha and ancestors every minute so that Daddy would heal. Don't let their act fool you. My parents were in love from the moment they met and are still in the thick of it, no matter how much they despise each other."* My mom's right. Mama must love Daddy to put up with all of his shit.

"Yes, Jayd, I still love your grandfather very much and tell your mama I said hi," Mama says, opening the door to the backhouse while simultaneously reading my mind. "I'm not mad at the other women in his life, either. I'm in no position to judge anyone," she says, claiming the mixing bowl already full of yellow batter and stirring it. "Life is untidy, to say the least. And nothing's ever what it seems. Your daddy's not a bad man. Just stupid." Mama smiles but I know she's serious.

"Why does Daddy cheat on you? Doesn't he know what he's got in you?" Mama stops mixing the batter and looks at her reflection in the silver bowl. I hope she sees the same thing I see: a beautiful black woman any man would be lucky to be with.

"Jayd, your grandfather is out there with those other women because they give him a sense of pride. They make him feel good in a way that I ceased doing long ago." Damn, Mama's so straight about the shit. I thought she'd break down and cry at the mention of her husband having other women, even though she has confronted them face-to-face on more than one occasion. I can learn from Mama a thing or two about controlling my emotions. I can't even stand the thought of Rah being with Trish or Sandy.

"If you know the problem, why don't you just fix it?" I ask, reading the directions on the kitchen table and gathering the ingredients needed to make the red hot water cornbread recipe for the festival on Friday. I asked Mama to show me how to make her special cornbread for my contribution to the club's menu, if we're able to participate. When I told Mama about Mrs. Bennett putting up a fight she assured me that Mr. Adewale's got everything under control. She also told me about this recipe and that if Mr. A eats this bread it'll fuel his fire, which will help us all prevail against our common enemy.

"I respect my husband's path, the way he hears God talk to him. I just wish he felt the same way about my path. And until he does that, I can't fix a damned thing," Mama says, forlornly staring out the window toward a memory I can't see. I think that's the first time this year I've heard Mama call Daddy her husband. "But enough about that," Mama says, taking the sock she was waving at Daddy from her dress pocket and tossing it into the kitchen sink. "We'll clean up my issues later. Let's fix your drama now, so we can get this club up and running. Our ancestors are waiting."

"I wish Misty would stop trying to ruin everything I touch," I say, putting salt into my bowl before pouring the cornmeal in the sifter, ready to repeat Mama's steps.

"Misty, Misty, Misty," Mama says. "Don't you get tired of saying that girl's name? Because I sure do get tired of hearing it." She pushes her batter aside to concentrate on mine. She takes six dried red chile peppers from a small bowl on the counter behind the table and crushes them in her hands. She then pours the peppers into my bowl.

"Of course I do. But she's always making trouble for me. I know she's behind Mrs. Bennett coming to our meeting last week and suddenly wanting to be our adviser. But I can't let that happen and I want to make sure the club is up and running so we can represent properly during the festival."

"Jayd, you're not a monkey in the circus. You don't have to jump through anyone's hoops for their culture day, or whatever it's called." Mama pours cayenne pepper into the batter as I get the hot water off the stove and slowly pour it into the mix. The heat from the peppers and the water is clearing my sinuses.

"I know you're right, but I don't want to let them win," I say, thinking of KJ, Reid, Misty, Laura, and the rest of the haters in my debate class who would love to see us fail.

"It's not a competition, baby." Mama puts her hand up for me to stop pouring and I replace the kettle on the stove.

"Then why does it feel like I'm constantly at war?" I look at Mama expertly eye the cornbread's texture. She takes the jar of honey on the table and pours a drop into the batter before blending.

"Because you keep fighting on their playing field instead of forcing them onto your own turf. Remember your dreams, Jayd. When you fought your enemies with your ancestors' sight you brought them to their knees. You can do the same here. Just believe in your power and it'll all work out, without you having to fight too hard. Trust me," she says, eyeing my batter. "When you're at school this week, ignore the drama around you and focus on your end result. I'm always telling you the same thing, young lady. When are you going to listen?"

Mama's right. If she can focus on her clients' issues and my shit while still dealing with all of the bull she and Daddy go through on the regular, I know I can, too. This will prove to be a powerful week if I can make it to Friday without going after Misty and her crew. But if being calm is what will help Mr. Adewale win over the administration, then that's exactly what I'm going to do.

Finally, the Cultural Awareness Festival is here. To start the special day off there's an assembly at the end of first period to explain the history behind the day, and that's where the performances will take place. All of our hard work is finally going to pay off. Chance and I have been rehearsing all week, with Nellie and Jeremy our eager audience. Who knew being in a club could be so much work and fun at the same time?

The most challenging part of starting the African Student Union was the opposition from the administration. Reid being up in arms about anything he didn't think of is nothing new. But Mrs. Bennett and her allies made it pretty clear that they didn't trust the motives of the club. Ain't that some bull? When Mr. Adewale found out about that, I made sure he ate an entire batch of Mama's cornbread, and I didn't even have to tell him they were from Mama. He already knew what was up since I was bringing him something to eat from home. And, as usual, it worked.

When Ms. Toni—who sits on several club committees and is the chair of ASB—said she never recalled the administration asking any of the other clubs what their motives were, Mrs. Bennett's white complexion turned crimson and so did her colleagues' faces. The only reason they had a problem with ASU is because it is by, about, and for the black students on this campus—a population they don't want riled up. But we're here and we're not going anywhere. And after a subtle threat from Mr. Adewale to take the issue public, they backed down and let us officially have our club.

Between the scene from *Fences* Chance and I are performing and the great menu at the festival this afternoon, the African Student Union's first outing should be a success—no thanks to most of the so-called members. At the end of the day, most of the work was done by our advisers, me, Nigel, and Chance. Even Emilio started to slack off after he realized he does not and will never have a chance with me. He's fine, but not my type, and it has nothing to do with race or culture. We just roll very differently and I can respect that. I hope that eventually Emilio can, too.

"How's my leading Lady J this morning?" Chance asks, giving me a hug as we exit the main parking lot in the front of the school. It's an exciting day and everyone's in a good mood. The overcast weather should burn off in time for the festival. I can't wait to get my multicultural grub on this afternoon. Last year every table had a spread worth sampling and plates are only three dollars—the maximum the school will allow for clubs to charge for food at campus fundraisers.

"Cute, real cute," I say, looking over my shoulder at Chance's Nova. Now that I've felt her horsepower I want to get behind the wheel again as soon as possible. I'm with my mom on this one: I'm only young once. Besides, I could've found much worse things to become addicted to. Gambling on races and all that ain't for me. But driving around on a clear night in a sweet hot rod is definitely part of my stylo now. "I'm good. How's my car?"

"Your car? I know you're not talking about my wife," he says, nudging me playfully as we make our way through the main gate. ASB members are running around like chickens with their heads cut off, throwing up red and white streamers everywhere as well as performing other last-minute busy tasks I hope I never have to do as a member of ASU. We're more of an intellectual club rather than a social butterfly type of network, and I for one hope it stays that way.

"Your wife, my car; same difference." I need to go to my locker before heading to Spanish class. Mr. Adewale couldn't care less about Cultural Awareness Day. In his class, Friday quizzes will still go down. "I'll see you in the auditorium."

"Alright, later Rose. I mean Jayd," Chance says, calling me by my character's name.

"Bye, Troy," I say, returning the love. How he's going to go in and out of character as first a Puritan slave owner, then a misunderstood black man, I don't know. But if anyone can do it, it's my boy. And it's a part of his destiny anyway. Chance smiles at me as he attempts to walk to his first class, but he's abruptly stopped by KJ, Del, and Money.

"We were talking about it and we've decided that we can't let you play a black man," KJ says, crossing his arms confidently across his Lakers jersey. Tonight must be game night. He always wears the basketball jersey for whatever team he's rooting for on the day of the game.

"He's more black than y'all will ever be," I say, defending my mixed friend, even if he doesn't know yet that he's got a little black in his blood. But this has gone far enough.

"What do you mean by that, Jayd? I know I'm white and I'm proud of it," Chance says. I wish I could tell him the truth, but it's not my place.

"Exactly. So now you understand our problem. Thank you and good day to you, sir," Del says, being the smart-ass he usually is.

"No, I don't understand. It's a play. No, actually it's one scene from a play and it's one of my favorites. I know this part like the back of my hand," Chance says, holding up his pale fist.

"And not one of you wanted the part. You have no right to harass Chance because he stepped up when you didn't." KJ looks down at me, snarling with his toothpick dangling from the side of his mouth. That's always been one of his most annoying habits, that and his cocky attitude.

"He's still not black, Jayd. But I don't think you'd know a black man if he was standing right in front of your face." KJ thinks he's funny but he's not.

"Whatever, KJ. You and I both know the truth about what a real black man is, don't we?" I say, causing oohs and ahhs to

ripple through the audience that has gathered, getting a pre-
view of our show to come. The scene Chance and I are performing is highly emotional and will no doubt captivate the
crowd, just like we're doing now. KJ probably would have
made a good Troy, but he's the one who messed that up, not
Chance.

"Really? Aren't you the same Jayd who's dating the white
boy? Oh no, wait, I think it's the Spanish dude this week," KJ
says. Money gives him dap as they get a good laugh in.

"I don't need his shit," Chance says, giving up and walking
back toward the parking lot. Oh no, he's not running away.
The show must go on, and it can't without Chance.

"Chance, don't listen to them," I say, catching up with him
and pulling his arm hard, forcing him to look at me. If my
eyes can work to get what I want any other time, why not
now? I stare into Chance's light brown eyes and begin to
melt away the anger and frustration I can feel in them. "You
can do this, Chance. You have every right to play this part.
It's in your blood," I say, convincing him without admitting
all that I know.

"You're right. I can do this," he says, now seeing things my
way. Mama's right—if I focus on my own powers, I can master them like my ancestors did with theirs. "Let's do this."

"That's what I'm talking about," I say, hugging my boy and
leading the way to class. I look back at KJ, Del, and Money,
feeling for their bruised egos. They should've stepped up in
the first place. Then they wouldn't be so hot about losing not
only another sistah to a white boy—as they would put it—
but also an opportunity to show what our people can do on-
stage. Most of the brothas I know consider theater acting a
gay or white thing, and that's their bad. Me and Chance are
going to honor August Wilson whether they like it or not.

Sometimes it's a black thing; sometimes it's a white thing.

Then sometimes it's just about doing the right thing. And I'm convinced that this is the right thing for me and my crew to do. Everyone else will have to worry about dealing with their culture shock on their own time, because we're about to do our thing.

Epilogue

Friday's events went off without another kink and because the scene went so well and the food was slamming, we raised enough money for our club so that we now need a bank account. The election of officers and other official club business will take place in the next week or so. This weekend is all about enjoying our victory, and that we did. My celebrating was cut short by my work schedule, as usual, but I still enjoyed hanging with my friends this weekend. Jeremy and I have been in a really good place lately and I'm looking forward to seeing just how far we take this love of ours.

I'm enjoying this Sunday afternoon by myself, eating my favorite food. I love chicken flavored Top Ramen with broccoli. The key is not cooking it too long. The noodles taste better with a little backbone in them. I'm also catching up on my television shows, including the new *90210*, even though I do get sick of those white girls complaining about life when they have the choice to chill. I'm saying, these broads have money, a nice crib, and their own rooms. They don't have to work and when they do, it's a plush job with hookups. When shit goes wrong in their lives it's all self-made.

"Jayd, it's me, Jeremy," my boo says through my mom's

front door. Here he goes, popping up again, but this time I
don't mind. I'm actually glad he came by.

"I'm coming," I say, hopping off the couch and opening
the door. I'm wearing my boy shorts and a tank top—not too
cute, but it'll do. At least I've already showered this morning,
unlike the last time he came by.

"I just wanted to say hi before the weekend is completely
gone," he says, kissing me on the cheek and coming in. "Cute
shorts."

"Thank you." I reach up and kiss Jeremy sweetly on the
lips and then fall into his warm embrace. "What's this?" I say,
taking the small bag from his hand and looking inside. It's a
voodoo doll. I look up at Jeremy, who's smiling. I'm not sure
how to react.

"It's supposed to be a peace offering, Miss Priestess. I just
want you to know that I dig you, however you get down. I
admit I was shocked when I found out, but I love you for all
that you are, voodoo priestess and all."

"Jeremy, I don't know what to say." He treats me like the
queen I am all the time, even when I'm not expecting it.

"Jayd, I want you back in my life, only you and only me.
Why do you keep fighting us?" Jeremy asks, bending down
and nibbling on my right ear. His soft lips send chills down
my spine. Instinctively, I return the affection, kissing him on
his neck. The faint scent of his cologne only attracts me more
to his tender spot. Jeremy shakes at the contact of my tongue
on his flesh. This fire between Jeremy and me is what always
gets us caught up.

"Jeremy, we're just not right for each other," I say, but
there's no use my protesting. He's got me right where he
wants me and I'm enjoying the surrender. I'll only let him go
so far before stopping our session.

"From where I'm standing, we're perfect for each other,"
Jeremy says, kissing me passionately, forcing me to lie back

on the couch to support the force. He's never been this fiery before. I guess seeing me with two guys this week was more than he could take. Men always want what they can't have. And maybe—just maybe—this time I'll give in to our mutual desire.

Drama High, Volume 10:

CULTURE CLASH

L. Divine

ABOUT THIS GUIDE

The following questions are intended to
enhance your group's reading of
DRAMA HIGH: CULTURE CLASH
by L. Divine.

DISCUSSION QUESTIONS

1. Should Jayd give up on Rah completely, even as a friend?
2. Would you date Jeremy even if you knew his parents were not hospitable to people of color? Should Jeremy be judged on his parents' beliefs or because of who he is?
3. Was Jayd wrong to cut Emilio completely off after his views of black Americans offended her? Do you think she should have been more understanding, or was Jayd justified in her reaction?
4. Would you be able to have an open dialogue about your religious beliefs at school? Why or why not?
5. Do you have a neighbor who seems a bit strange to you? What types of differences make this person stand apart in your neighborhood? Outside of these differences, are you more alike than not?
6. Were KJ and his boys justified in their response to Chance taking a black role? What do you think should have been done differently, if anything?
7. Should Jayd resume her relationship with Jeremy and leave Rah alone? Do you think their cultural differences will get in the way of their second chance, or have they both learned enough about each other by now to make it work this time?

8. Does your school have an African Student Union? If not, would you consider starting one? What would be the purpose of your club?

9. Was Nigel's mom right about Mickey having an abortion? Do you think Nigel and Mickey should live together once the baby's born?

10. Is Rah handling his baby-mama situation in the most effective manner? What could he do differently to make the situation better for himself, his daughter, and for Jayd?

Jaydism #2

When Ms. Toni wanted to communicate with Jayd but fell short of knowing exactly what she wanted to say, she picked a novel to do the talking for her. The next time you want to share something about yourself or your feelings, use one of your favorite books to get your message across. You might be surprised by how well this works in making your point without arguing.

Stay tuned for the next book in
the DRAMA HIGH series,
COLD AS ICE

Until then, satisfy your DRAMA HIGH craving
with the following excerpt from the next
exciting installment

ENJOY!

Prologue

The tickle down the right side of my neck distracts me from keeping up with the steady pace of Jeremy's lips. He started out kissing my left ear and then moved on to my right. Now Jeremy's focus has returned to my mouth and I'm glad for it. I love the way his soft lips feel against mine, even though him kissing my neck is definitely my next favorite thing. I could lie on this couch with him forever as long as he keeps making me feel this good.

Jeremy and I have been making out for what seems like hours, but I'm not worried about the time. My phone's gone off twice since he got here and I could not care less. I know it's Rah, ready to grill me about seeing Jeremy kiss me on Friday night at the race, but I have nothing to say to him about what we do. I just hope we don't stop anytime soon. The second time around for Jeremy and me just might be what we both need.

"I'll give you a thousand dollars for that thought," Jeremy says, pulling away from my lips and promptly kissing me on my nose. We both need to come up for air, but not for long I hope. It's been a while since I had a make-out session without having to look over my shoulder for a crazy ex-girlfriend or baby-mama in attack mode.

"And you probably would, too," I say, kissing Jeremy on his neck—and by the way, he's shaking. I can tell he likes it. I keep kissing, softly biting his flesh as I smile at every involuntary jump he makes.

"Come on, Jayd. I'm serious," Jeremy says, kissing me on my right cheek and then again on my ear. If he doesn't stop we're going to get into some serious trouble that I know I'm not ready for. I'll be seventeen next month, and all of my friends are waiting on me to lose my virginity—since I'm the last one in our crew and probably the whole damn school. But I'm not going out like that—not yet. "From now on we need to have full disclosure—no secrets. That's the only way this can work."

"Full disclosure? I'm not sure I can do that," I say, easing my way up from under him and sitting up straight on the small couch that doubles as my weekend bed. The couch was already a mess before Jeremy got here and now it looks like a tornado hit it. The pillows are strewn across the living room floor with my sheets and blanket across the coffee table. If my mom walked in right now she'd be more upset by the mess in her apartment than the boy making out with her daughter.

"Why not?" Jeremy asks in that innocent way of his that makes my heart melt. He's so adorable when he's on a mission for information. "Look, Jayd, I'm serious about having a committed relationship with you, and that means we have to be completely honest with each other, even if it means having to hear something we might not want to. So, what's on your mind?" I look into Jeremy's blue eyes and see his sincerity. But I still don't feel comfortable telling him everything about how me, Mama, and my mom get down.

"Because, Jeremy, there are some things I can never tell you or anyone else about my life," I say as Jeremy sits up next to me. "It's not that I don't want to tell you, or that I'm keeping anything from you on purpose. It's just the way it is. I

hope you can understand." I really, really do. Me being a priestess is a big adjustment for Jeremy, I know. But it's a non-
negotiable part of my life that all of my friends have learned
to deal with in one way or another.

"I can respect that, Lady J. I can't help but hope that one
day you can tell me everything, no holds barred." Jeremy
pulls me into his arms again and I accept his warm embrace.
He always smells fresh, like Irish Spring and seawater. It
must be from all the surfing he does on a daily basis. "Anyway, I have to get going. I'm meeting the gang at the pier and
still need to get my boards from my bro," he says, kissing me
on the back of the neck before letting me go.

"Not yet," I say, rising with him. "We've got all day." I know
I have a ton of things to do before I head back to Compton
this evening, but all of that can wait if he'll stay.

"Ah, baby, I wish I could stay and hang, but we have a surfing competition coming up and we're in need of some serious practice." I never knew surfing was more than a hobby to
Jeremy. I had no idea he competed outside of his crew, just
like I didn't know about him and Chance drag racing for money.
It seems like I have a lot to learn about my elusive friend.

"Full disclosure, huh? You have a few secrets of your own
I'm not privy to, don't you, Mr. Weiner?" I ask, pushing him
in his lower back as we walk to the front door. He's got a
cute butt for a white boy, and I love his strong, tanned legs,
even if they are covered in hair.

"We all do. But for you, Miss Jackson, I'll be an open book."
Jeremy turns around and strokes my face with the back of his
right hand before bending down for one last kiss. I gently
grab the back of his head, entangling my fingers in his thick
curls. Jeremy's hands move from my face down to my waist
and he pulls me in closer. Here we go again.

"Damn. Do you have to go now?" I whine as he releases
me from his embrace. Jeremy opens the door and steps over

the threshold, officially ending our make-up make-out afternoon. Every time Jeremy kisses me like this I feel swept away in the moment. This fool's got some power over me and we both know it.

"I love you too, Jayd," Jeremy says, kissing me on the forehead and jogging down the stairs without allowing me to respond. That fool just said he loved me and ran off. What the hell?

I step back inside and close the door as my phone rings once again. I push the silence button and notice the time, realizing I need to get a move on. I just remembered I was supposed to meet my crew at Nigel's house about an hour ago. No wonder Rah's been texting and calling me like crazy. I completely lost track of time, but that's how it is once Jeremy and I get started—and I don't regret a single minute.

While relocking the multiple bolts on my mom's front door, I swear I can feel someone's eyes on me. I walk over to the living room window and look outside over the neighbor's tall trees to see if I notice anyone staring my way. I don't have time to play 007 right now. I have to clean up this place and get ready to go, which includes a shower and doing my hair. It's still early in the afternoon and I know my crew's not going anywhere anytime soon. I'll be there as soon as I can, but I'm not rushing for anyone. Besides, I feel too good from Jeremy's surprise visit and love confession to care about being late or about who may be spying on us. I just want to enjoy this feeling a little while longer before I have to deal with my crew and their inevitable issues.

~ 1 ~
The Ultimate Betrayal

*"Yuh need fi check yuhself before yuh start kiss yuh teeth/
Caw yuh nuh ready fi this yet bwoy."*

—TANYA STEPHENS

Once all of my chores were done at my mom's apartment, I gave my hair a quick wash and dry before flat-ironing it and packing my stuff. It's been a minute since I've had time to give my hair the proper love and care it deserves, but hopefully next weekend I'll have more time to pamper myself. I sent Mickey a text a few minutes ago, informing her I was on my way. I don't even know why I'm going to this session. I have schoolwork to catch up on and there are always Mama's assignments to do. Will a sistah ever get a break?

When I pull up to Nigel's house I see all of my friends are in attendance this sunny Sunday afternoon. I wish I were at the beach with Jeremy, as nice as the weather is. I park my little gray ride behind Chance's Chevy and turn off the engine. Maybe I can take Chance's car around the block before we leave and disturb Nigel's pristine neighborhood. I need to make it a habit to drive his and Jeremy's cars more often, so I can sharpen my hot-rod driving skills. I wonder if girls ever race in their car crew?

"Sorry I'm late, y'all. What did I miss?" I ask, entering Nigel's foyer and greeting my friends chilling in the plush living room. They all look distracted by whatever's on the flat screen television. I'm surprised Mickey would come back so soon after

Mrs. Esop called her out last week about being unsure of the paternity of her unborn child. But I guess my girl's still hopeful she'll be accepted into the family. If there ever was an eternal optimist in the midst of the darkest of challenges, it's Mickey. She's dead set on marrying Nigel and becoming a housewife, even if his mama can't stand her.

"Damn, Jayd. You missed everything. Me and Nellie are almost done with the registry and guest list," Mickey says, flipping through baby catalogues, which has been her and Nellie's favorite pastime lately. I'll be so glad when this baby is born I won't know what to do. I walk into the living room and join the session in progress. I know they didn't smoke down here, but my boys are definitely on cloud nine.

"You must've been real busy to be almost three hours late. Where were you?" Nellie asks, tagging several pages with pink Post-It notes. Party planning is definitely my girl's thing. Maybe she can plan a small birthday celebration for me this year. My birthdays are usually uneventful, but I wouldn't mind doing a little something on my special day. Nigel and Chance nod their greetings without looking away from the Chow Yun-Fat flick in front of them. Martial arts always mesmerize my boys, and he is one of my favorite actors, too. Looks like I came just in time, no matter what Nellie and Mickey may think.

"She was with her boy toy," Rah says, taking his red eyes away from the fight scene on the big screen to glare at me. I knew he would be irritated about seeing Jeremy kiss me on Friday, but he really can't say shit. I have to endure not one but two of his ex-heffas sniffing around him on the regular. Jeremy and I actually have a future together, unlike what he and Trish and Sandy have.

"He's not my boy toy," I say, ready to defend me and Jeremy if need be. "I know you know me better than that, Rah," I say, rolling my eyes at him and sitting down next to Nellie on the couch. Mickey and Nigel are cuddled up together on the loveseat and Chance is sitting on the floor in front of Nellie while she plays in his hair. Everyone's coupled off except for me and Rah, yet we're the two that brought them all together. Isn't this ironic?

"Then what is he, Jayd?" Rah asks, turning his body around to face me completely in the chair he's posted up in next to the couch. "You're usually not late to a session and you didn't answer my calls or texts. Naturally I got worried and went by to check on you. Before I could get out of the car I saw your boy Jeremy leaving your mom's apartment, and he looked very happy," Rah says, waiting for my confession—but from where I'm sitting I don't owe him an explanation.

"Ooh, a midafternoon make-out session. I love it," Nellie says, taking her hands out of Chance's hair and clapping. "Details, please." Nellie is a bit too excited for the heaviness of the situation between me and Rah. I'll fill her in on the kiss-by-kiss encounter another time. Right now I need to check my boy before he goes too far.

"Rah, Jeremy and I are friends, and you've known that all along. Besides, you don't see me spying on your ass when you don't answer my calls, which is quite often now that Sandy's back in your life," I say, sucking my teeth at him. He's got nerve enough for the both of us.

"Jayd, you can say whatever you like, but you know you're wrong to be dealing with that punk again. He shouldn't even be touching you," Rah says, his high cheekbones flexing at the very thought of Jeremy and me kissing. I didn't mean for him to ever witness Jeremy and me being affectionate, but it happened and there's no going back.

"Hey, that punk is my friend, and he helped you win that basketball game against KJ, don't forget," Chance says, having Jeremy's back like a true homie. Nigel has his back, too, but he's Rah's homie first, so he's silent for the time being. But I know if Rah gets too carried away Nigel will step in. We all know Rah's not really pissed at Jeremy; he's just jealous because I'm doing my own thing.

"Whatever, man," Rah says, calming down for the time being, or so I think. After a few minutes of silence, Rah comes back at me. Am I going to get to watch the movie in peace, or what?

"Just admit that the shit was disrespectful, Jayd, and I'll let it go." Mickey and Nellie look at Rah and then back at me. Nigel feels the gravity of the situation and turns the volume down on the surround-sound system his dad hooked up in here, much to Chance's disapproval. The entertainment system in the game room is even tighter than this one and I already feel like I'm at one of Magic Johnson's theaters. But Rah's drama is distracting us all from watching the movie.

"I'm not admitting a damn thing," I say, now just as irritated as Rah. This fool is really tripping and messing up my vibe. I was feeling good when I left my mom's house. Now I feel like kicking his ass. "Can you please shut up so we can enjoy the movie? We'll talk about it later." If I were a dude Rah would've socked me in my mouth for telling him to be quiet. He looks like he's going to hit something and I feel him.

"You've lost your damn mind, you know that?" Rah says, standing up from his seat and towering over me. "Do you really think I'm stupid, Jayd? I know you and that punk-ass white boy are more than friends—no offense, man," Rah says to Chance, who looks like he wants to jump in, but chooses against it. When Rah gets this angry there's no reasoning with him. Nigel gets up from his cozy spot next to Mickey just in case he needs to cool Rah down.

"Come on, man. Let's take a walk," Nigel says, trying to distract Rah. But Rah's eyes are set on me, and mine on him. Nellie scoots over, putting more space between her leg and mine. Chance scoots over on the floor just in case Rah takes another step and accidentally crushes Chance's fingers underneath his new Jordans.

"You betrayed me, Jayd. You betrayed us," Rah says between his teeth before storming out of the living room and through front door, passing Mr. and Mrs. Esop on his way down the porch steps. Nigel looks down at me and shrugs his shoulders before following his boy. I haven't seen Rah this angry with me in a long time.

"Rah, wait a minute. It's not that serious," I say, rising to follow them out. He can be so dramatic sometimes.

"Hello, Jayd," Mrs. Esop says, leading her husband through the open door. I smile at Nigel's mom and dad before walking through the foyer. They look stunning in their Sunday best, fresh from church.

"What's wrong with Rah?" Mr. Esop asks, turning his head to watch Rah start his car before heading to the game room next to the living room. Mrs. Esop takes off her large white hat and smoothes her hair down in the antique mirror hanging in the entryway.

"Oh, the usual," I say, looking back at my crew looking at us instead of the muted screen in front of them. A live show is always more interesting. "I'll be right back," I say, adjusting my purse on my shoulder and walking down the steps. I'm so sick of doing damage control, but it's an inevitable part of maintaining friendships. And sometimes boys can be more difficult to deal with than girls when it comes to matters of the heart.

"Jayd, I'm looking forward to continuing our discussion soon about becoming a debutante," Mrs. Esop says. I thought I was out of that deal when she went off on Mickey.

"But I just assumed you wouldn't be interested any longer in coming to the shower," I say, trying to speak low so Mickey doesn't hear. I haven't told her about my deal with Mrs. Esop yet. But from the look on her crooked face, I'd say Mickey heard the entire conversation. Shit. Now I'll have to deal with her drama, too.

"Just because it's not my grandchild doesn't mean that I can't enjoy the festivities," she says with a cunning smile. "And I am nothing if not a woman of my word. Besides, a deal's a deal," Mrs. Esop says, waving to Mickey, Nellie, and Chance before walking up the stairs. Mickey looks at me like she's about to explode she's so pissed, but I'll have to deal with her later. Right now I have to catch Rah before he does something stupid, which is the usual when his head gets this hot. Why does my life have to include all of this bull?

START YOUR OWN BOOK CLUB

Courtesy of the DRAMA HIGH series

ABOUT THIS GUIDE

The following is intended to help you get
the book club you've always wanted
up and running!
Enjoy!

Start Your Own Book Club

A Book Club is not only a great way to make friends, but it is also a fun and safe environment for you to express your views and opinions on everything from fashion to teen pregnancy. A Teen Book Club can also become a forum or venue to air grievances and plan remedies for problems.

The People

To start, all you need is yourself and at least one other person. There's no criteria for who this person or persons should be other than their having a desire to read and a commitment to discuss things during a certain time frame.

The Rules

Just as in Jayd's life, sometimes even Book Club discussions can be filled with much drama. People tend to disagree with each other, cut each other off when speaking, and take criticism personally. So, there should be some ground rules:

1. Do not attack people for their ideas or opinions.
2. When you disagree with a Book Club member on a point, disagree respectfully. This means that you do not denigrate other people or their ideas, i.e., no name-calling or saying, "That's stupid!" Instead, say, "I can respect your position; however, I feel differently."
3. Back up your opinions with concrete evidence, either from the book in question or life in general.
4. Allow everyone a turn to comment.
5. Do not cut a member off when the person is speaking. Respectfully wait your turn.
6. Critique only the idea. Do not criticize the person.

7. Every member must agree to and abide by the ground rules.

Feel free to add any other ground rules you think might be necessary.

The Meeting Place

Once you've decided on members, and agreed to the ground rules, you should decide on a place to meet. This could be the local library, the school library, your favorite restaurant, a bookstore, or a member's home. Remember, though, if you decide to hold your sessions at a member's home, the location should rotate to another member's home for the next session. It's also polite for guests to bring treats when attending a Book Club meeting at a member's home. If you choose to hold your meetings in a public place, always remember to ask the permission of the librarian or store manager. If you decide to hold your meetings in a local bookstore, ask the manager to post a flyer in the window announcing the Book Club to attract more members if you so desire.

Timing Is Everything

Teenagers of today are all much busier than teenagers of the past. You're probably thinking, "Between chorus rehearsals, the Drama Club, and oh yeah, my job, when will I ever have time to read another book that doesn't feature Romeo and Juliet!" Well, there's always time, if it's time well-planned and time planned ahead. You and your Book Club can decide to meet as often or as little as is appropriate for your bustling schedules. *Once a month* is a favorite option. *Sleepover Book Club* meetings—if you're open to excluding one gender—is also a favorite option. And in this day of high-tech, savvy teens, *Internet Discussion Groups* are also an appealing option. Just choose what's right for you!

Well, you've got the people, the ground rules, the place, and the time. All you need now is a book!

The Book

Choosing a book is the most fun. CULTURE CLASH is of course an excellent choice, and since it's part of a series, you won't soon run out of books to read and discuss. Your Book Club can also have comparative discussions as you compare the first book, THE FIGHT, to the second, SECOND CHANCE, and so on.

But depending upon your reading appetite, you may want to veer outside of the Drama High series. That's okay. There are plenty of options, many of which you will be able to find under the Dafina Books for Young Readers Program in the coming months.

But don't be afraid to mix it up. Nonfiction is just as good as fiction and a fun way to learn about from where we came without just using a history textbook. Science fiction and fantasy can be fun, too!

And always, always research the author. You might find that the author has a Web site where you can post your Book Club's questions or comments. The author may even have an e-mail address available so you can correspond directly. Authors might also sit in on your Book Club meetings, either in person, or on the phone, and this can be a fun way to discuss the book as well!

The Discussion

Every good Book Club discussion starts with questions. CULTURE CLASH, as does every book in the Drama High series, comes with a Reading Group Guide for your convenience, though of course, it's fine to make up your own. Here are some sample questions to get started:

1. What's this book all about anyway?
2. Who are the characters? Do we like them? Do they remind us of real people?
3. Was the story interesting? Were real issues that are of concern to you examined?
4. Were there details that didn't quite work for you or ring true?
5. Did the author create a believable environment—one that you could visualize?
6. Was the ending satisfying?
7. Would you read another book from this author?

Record Keeper

It's generally a good idea to have someone keep track of the books you read. Often libraries and schools will hold reading drives where you're rewarded for having read a certain number of books in a certain time period. Perhaps a pizza party awaits!

Get Your Teachers and Parents Involved

Teachers and parents love it when kids get together and read. So involve your teachers and parents. Your Book Club may read a particular book whereby it would help to have an adult's perspective as part of the discussion. Teachers may also be able to include what you're doing as a Book Club in the classroom curriculum. That way, books you love to read, such as the Drama High ones, can find a place in your classroom alongside the books you don't love to read so much.

Resources

To find some new favorite writers, check out the following resources. Happy reading!

Young Adult Library Services Association
http://www.ala.org/ala/yalsa/yalsa.htm

Carnegie Library of Pittsburgh
Hip-Hop!
Teen Rap Titles
http://www.carnegielibrary.org/teens/read/booklists/teen rap.html

TeensPoint.org
What Teens Are Reading
http://www.teenspoint.org/reading_matters/book_list.asp?s ort=5&list=274

Teenreads.com
http://www.teenreads.com

Sacramento Public Library
Fantasy Reading for Kids
http://www.saclibrary.org/teens/fantasy.html

Book Divas
http://www.bookdivas.com

Meg Cabot Book Club
http://www.megcabotbookclub.com